American Soldiers

by Matt Morillo

A Samuel French Acting Edition

New York Hollywood London Toronto

SAMUELFRENCH.COM

Copyright © 2010 by Matt Morillo

ALL RIGHTS RESERVED

Cover artwork designed by Suzanne Yoda

CAUTION: Professionals and amateurs are hereby warned that *AMERICAN SOLDIERS* is subject to a Licensing Fee. It is fully protected under the copyright laws of the United States of America, the British Commonwealth, including Canada, and all other countries of the Copyright Union. All rights, including professional, amateur, motion picture, recitation, lecturing, public reading, radio broadcasting, television and the rights of translation into foreign languages are strictly reserved. In its present form the play is dedicated to the reading public only.

The amateur and professional live stage performance rights to *AMERICAN SOLDIERS* are controlled exclusively by Samuel French, Inc., and licensing arrangements and performance licenses must be secured well in advance of presentation. PLEASE NOTE that amateur Licensing Fees are set upon application in accordance with your producing circumstances. When applying for a licensing quotation and a performance license please give us the number of performances intended, dates of production, your seating capacity and admission fee. Licensing Fees are payable one week before the opening performance of the play to Samuel French, Inc., at 45 W. 25th Street, New York, NY 10010.

Licensing Fee of the required amount must be paid whether the play is presented for charity or gain and whether or not admission is charged.

Professional/Stock licensing fees quoted upon application to Samuel French, Inc.

For all other rights than those stipulated above, apply to: KADM Productions, kadmproductions@yahoo.com.

Particular emphasis is laid on the question of amateur or professional readings, permission and terms for which must be secured in writing from Samuel French, Inc.

Copying from this book in whole or in part is strictly forbidden by law, and the right of performance is not transferable.

Whenever the play is produced the following notice must appear on all programs, printing and advertising for the play: "Produced by special arrangement with Samuel French, Inc."

Due authorship credit must be given on all programs, printing and advertising for the play.

ISBN 978-0-573-69862-0   Printed in U.S.A.   #29620

No one shall commit or authorize any act or omission by which the copyright of, or the right to copyright, this play may be impaired.

No one shall make any changes in this play for the purpose of production.

Publication of this play does not imply availability for performance. Both amateurs and professionals considering a production are strongly advised in their own interests to apply to Samuel French, Inc., for written permission before starting rehearsals, advertising, or booking a theatre.

No part of this book may be reproduced, stored in a retrieval system, or transmitted in any form, by any means, now known or yet to be invented, including mechanical, electronic, photocopying, recording, videotaping, or otherwise, without the prior written permission of the publisher.

MUSIC USE NOTE

Licensees are solely responsible for obtaining formal written permission from copyright owners to use copyrighted music in the performance of this play and are strongly cautioned to do so. If no such permission is obtained by the licensee, then the licensee must use only original music that the licensee owns and controls. Licensees are solely responsible and liable for all music clearances and shall indemnify the copyright owners of the play and their licensing agent, Samuel French, Inc., against any costs, expenses, losses and liabilities arising from the use of music by licensees.

IMPORTANT BILLING AND CREDIT REQUIREMENTS

All producers of *AMERICAN SOLDIERS must* give credit to the Author of the Play in all programs distributed in connection with performances of the Play, and in all instances in which the title of the Play appears for the purposes of advertising, publicizing or otherwise exploiting the Play and/or a production. The name of the Author *must* appear on a separate line on which no other name appears, immediately following the title and *must* appear in size of type not less than fifty percent of the size of the title type.

EXTRA SPECIAL ACKNOWLEDGMENT
Crystal Field
and
Theater for the New City

Once again we find ourselves indebted to Crystal Field and all the wonderful people at Theater for the New City (TNC). With the success of *Angry Young Women In Low Rise Jeans With High Class Issues* and *All Aboard the Marriage Hearse*, both light-hearted comedies, Crystal and TNC allowed us to explore and grow in a new direction with *American Soldiers*. This production was a wonderful experience and allowed us to show some versatility that we hope will be a trademark of all of our future productions.

Once again Crystal and TNC showed that they are true supporters of the arts. We cannot thank them enough for their continued support.

Organizations like TNC are very difficult to find, organizations that nurture emerging artists and allow them to grow in a creative environment. They have helped launched the careers of many great, well-known playwrights, actors, and artists of all kinds.

Once again, a great many thanks to Crystal Field and Theater for the New City. Please support this organization. They are doing some amazing things.

For more information about TNC, visit:
www.theaterforthenewcity.net

SPECIAL THANKS

Richard West, PIP Printing of Hicksville, SuperGrip, Kenny Yee, Michael Sgouros, Michaelangelo Alassa, Tony Ruiz, Duo Theater, NYC, Junior Gonzalez, The Players Theater, the McGill Family, Suzanne Gorney-Yoda, Pete Yoda, The Hicksivlle Crew, Mark Marcante, Jonathan Weber, Candice Burridge, Chris Force, Jon D. Andreadakis, Richard Reta, Francesse Maingrette, Lissa Moira, Alex Bartenieff, Bob Homeyer, Zen Mansely, and a thank you to all our friends and family for their support!

And of course, a thank you to the late great Jerry Jaffe...you are missed!

This play is dedicated to the memory of Vivek Adarkar. Thanks for the training, the conversation, the good times and the support during the 'carefree college days' and after. You were a great mentor. I wish you could be here to see this one... and all the ones that follow.
I miss you, my friend. This one is for you!

AMERICAN SOLDIERS was first produced from January 14th through January 31st of 2010 at the Theater for the New City at 155 1st Avenue in New York City.

CARLO COLLETTI SR.	Stu Richel
ANGELA COLLETTI	Kate Reilly
CARLO COLLETTI JR.	Tom Pilutik
MARIE COLLETTI	Julia Giolzetti
JONATHAN "HUTCH" HUTCHINSON	Nick Coleman

Producers	Matt Morillo, Nick Coleman, and Tom Pilutik
Assistant Director	Nick Coleman
Set Design	Mark Marcante
Lighting Design	Amith A. Chandrashaker
Publicity	Jonathan Slaff and Associates
Cover Art	Suzanne Yoda
Graphic Design	Kenneth Yee ky.arts@gmail.com

NOTES FOR PRODUCERS

Credit for the playwright should be as follows:

Filmmaker/Playwright Matt Morillo has also written *Angry Young Women in Low Rise Jeans With High Class Issues* and *All Aboard the Marriage Hearse* and both are published by Samuel French, Inc. He is also an award-winning filmmaker. For more info on him, visit his websites, Kadm.com, AngryYoungWomen.net and TheCynicalOptimist.net.

In the event that producers are required to cast a non-overweight actor as Carlo Sr., they should feel free to remove the references to his overeating, but MAY NOT remove any references to his drinking.

In the event of budget constraints, producers should not feel obligated to erect an entire set, just get the integral pieces and improvise the rest.

CHARACTERS

CARLO COLLETTI SR.– Early sixties, burnt-out, slightly overweight, hard-drinking, ex-cop and Vietnam Veteran. Basically a good guy but can be abrasive at times as he's struggling with being a widower and his eldest daughter returning from serving a traumatic tour in Iraq.

ANGELA COLLETTI– Late twenties, was once an idealistic young woman with political aspirations, but she enlisted in the Army, lost a fianceé, and witnessed many awful incidents, leaving her scarred. Her experiences have left her unable to believe in anything she believed in before she left.

CARLO COLLETTI JR. (JUNIOR)– Early thirties, handsome, idealistic young politician. Struggles with being a Democrat in a heavy Republican area. Good family man who is just trying to keep his family together because he believes his father no longer can.

MARIE COLLETTI– Early twenties, youngest of the Colletti family. A pretty, party girl who has been stuck watching her father's slow deterioration after her mother's death. Her struggles are enhanced by Angela's return home, which only causes her father more stress.

JONATHAN "HUTCH" HUTCHINSON– Late twenties, affable "town drunk" and ne'er do well. He's Angela's ex-boyfriend and the only one who tried to talk her out of enlisting years back. He's a bit of a Nihilist and loves to pretend to be stupid while he criticizes the "establishment" on Long Island.

SETTING

The kitchen of an upper-middle class house in Hicksville, Long Island, New York.

TIME

Around 12:30 a.m. on an evening in early September, just around Labor Day.

ACT I

Scene I

(A large, cluttered suburban kitchen replete with a refrigerator, a stove with a light above it, a counter, cabinets, a sink and in the center of the room, a table. On the backstage wall, above the sink, is a window with curtains. There is a door at stage right that leads to an offstage living room, a door and screen door at stage left that leads to an offstage backyard. The decor is modern, yet has a slightly old fashioned feel.)

(The lights come up on the kitchen. **CARLO SR.**, *sporting a two-day growth, sits at the kitchen table with a blank look on his face.)*

(He gets up and goes over to the cabinet and pulls out a bottle of whiskey.)

(He pours himself a glass.)

(He brings the bottle and the glass over to the table as he retakes his seat.)

(We hear footsteps offstage.)

*(***CARLO SR.*** gets very excited.)*

(He gets up and faces the backyard door.)

*(***JUNIOR*** enters from the living room door.)*

JUNIOR. What's up, pop?

CARLO SR. Oh, it's you.

JUNIOR. Nice to see you too.

CARLO SR. Stop that. You know I didn't mean anything by it.

JUNIOR. I don't know that actually.

CARLO SR. I said to stop that.

JUNIOR. So she's still not here?

CARLO SR. You don't see her, do you?

JUNIOR. Dad, calm down.

CARLO SR. I'm calm.

JUNIOR. No you're not so why don't you go to bed and relax?

CARLO SR. I'll relax right here.

*(He goes to pour more whiskey but **JUNIOR** grabs it right before he gets it to the glass.)*

Don't ever take that out of my hands again.

JUNIOR. Don't ever pick it up again and I won't.

CARLO SR. Go home, Carlo.

JUNIOR. Seriously. Go to bed.

CARLO SR. Seriously. I'm staying right here. My house. My kitchen.

*(**CARLO SR.** grabs the bottle again. **JUNIOR** grabs at it and they tug of war over it a little.)*

Did you ever think I might want to have a celebratory toast with my daughter when she walks in?

JUNIOR. I don't think so at all.

*(**JUNIOR** wrests the bottle away and returns it to the cabinet.)*

CARLO SR. I took that out two seconds before you walked in, so you can call off your crusade.

JUNIOR. I don't buy that for a second.

CARLO SR. I really don't give a damn what you buy and I want you to go home.

JUNIOR. You're going to bed and I'm going to wait up for her.

CARLO SR. It's best if I'm the one to greet her.

JUNIOR. You look like shit, you smell like booze and...what happened here? Did you run out of razors?

CARLO SR. I'm not running for office, dipshit. I don't need to shave everyday.

JUNIOR. Are you at least going to shave for the Christening?

CARLO SR. Shut up and get out of here.

JUNIOR. No.

CARLO SR. Oh Christ. You know what? No one is going to wait up for her. You're going home and I'm going to bed.

*(**CARLO SR.** tries to push **JUNIOR** towards the door but he doesn't budge. **SENIOR** gives up.)*

She's doing this on purpose. She obviously doesn't want all this fanfare for her return. She's made that clear.

JUNIOR. Dad, stop.

CARLO SR. I bet she doesn't show again.

JUNIOR. She'll show this time. I'm sure of it. Don't make this any harder than it is.

CARLO SR. Just go home and if she shows up we'll all just see her tomorrow. Sound good?

JUNIOR. Sounds bad. I'll just –

CARLO SR. I said go home!

JUNIOR. You go up to bed! Marie called me and said you've been on edge all day. Now enough is enough.

CARLO SR. What does she know? She's a twenty-two year-old kid.

JUNIOR. And in the past three minutes you've done nothing to convince me she's wrong.

CARLO SR. Don't you have a wife and kids who miss you? Let me try that again, don't you have a wife and kids?

JUNIOR. They're sleeping. Which is exactly where you should be.

CARLO SR. Alright you stubborn son of a bitch. You want this, you got it. You can wait up for her. I keep forgetting that you're the genius who knows how to handle all situations and that you're the right man for this job. I don't know what my problem is.

JUNIOR. Probably the whiskey. Now go get some rest and calm yourself down.

CARLO SR. I want some water first.

(**CARLO SR.** *grabs a pitcher of water from the fridge and takes a gulp.*)

JUNIOR. Why bother? You're going to have to get up and piss it out in fifteen minutes anyway.

CARLO SR. Don't be here when I do.

(**SENIOR** *starts for the door.*)

JUNIOR. Happy birthday by the way.

CARLO SR. It's not until tomorrow.

JUNIOR. It's after midnight.

CARLO SR. Know it all.

(**CARLO SR.** *reaches the door. He's about to leave the kitchen, but he stops.* **JUNIOR** *doesn't seem to notice.*)

(**CARLO SR.** *sneaks up behind him and smacks him in the back of the head.*)

JUNIOR. What the hell was that for?

CARLO SR. Don't give her any grief. You understand?

JUNIOR. What is your problem?

CARLO SR. I will dig out my gun and shoot you if you mess with her.

JUNIOR. Mess with her?

(**JUNIOR**'s *cell phone rings.*)

CARLO SR. Good. There's your wife. She wants you home.

(**JUNIOR** *silences the phone and doesn't answer.*)

JUNIOR. I'm not going anywhere. Now go.

CARLO SR. Just…just don't make her feel anything but welcome. Got it?

JUNIOR. I will be so nice and pretend everything is back to normal.

CARLO SR. You sure are an expert at that. Just like your mother.

*(**CARLO SR.** leaves.)*

*(**JUNIOR** jumps up from his seat and turns off the lights.)*

(He picks up his phone and dials.)

(He performs the following action as he talks on the cell.)

JUNIOR. Hey honey. Sorry about that, he was in one of his moods. Hopefully not very long… I will…I'll tell her…

(He peers out the window as if he sees something, being very sneaky.)

I'm sure she can't wait to see you and the girls too… Okay. Gotta go…Love you.

(He hangs up as someone appears at the back door.)

*(It's **ANGELA**.)*

*(He runs over to the living room door and hides in it, so that **ANGELA** can't see him.)*

(She enters the kitchen, carrying a huge duffle bag.)

(She doesn't notice him in the darkness.)

(He steps out and flicks the lights back on.)

(That startles her a little bit. She looks over at him with no smile.)

Hello.

*(No response from **ANGELA**. She still seems a bit startled. He moves over and gives her a very tight hug.)*

(He relaxes the hug and pulls back to look her in the face.)

I'm so glad you're home. It's…you know…forget it. You okay?

ANGELA. I didn't know you were here.

(He picks up her bag.)

JUNIOR. I came in through the front. Whoa. This is heavy. Why didn't you let any of us come get you? Have a seat. I'll take this upstairs for you.

ANGELA. No, no. Leave it. I'll take it.

JUNIOR. I'll do it.

ANGELA. That's okay. Thanks. Just leave it there please.

JUNIOR. Okay. Let me get you a beer.

ANGELA. Don't bother. I have to change and head out.

(She picks up her bag and starts for the living room door. He stops her.)

JUNIOR. But you just got here.

ANGELA. I'm meeting Hutch at one thirty.

JUNIOR. Hutch? Meet him tomorrow.

ANGELA. I want to see him tonight.

*(She starts to leave the room again and **JUNIOR** stops her again.)*

JUNIOR. Wait. Hang out with me for a few minutes. Come on.

(He goes for the beers.)

ANGELA. Carlo, I came in just to drop my bag off and change.

JUNIOR. Hang with me for a bit, and I'll give you a lift.

ANGELA. I can walk.

JUNIOR. But I already have the beers out.

ANGELA. Put them back.

(He cracks them open.)

JUNIOR. Too late. Come on, pre-game with me. One beer. I need it too. I've been planning a goddamn Christening all week.

(She reluctantly drops her bag and accepts the beer. He taps her beer bottle with his.)

Good to have you home.

(She sips her beer, not looking too happy.)

JUNIOR. *(cont.)* That's the spirit. Sorry all we have is light beer. We're trying to get Dad to cut down a bit. We've even watered down his whiskey bottles. Don't tell him.

(JUNIOR *sits. She doesn't.*)

Sit. This will be quick. How late do you think I can stay up?

ANGELA. What do you want to talk to me about?

JUNIOR. Why does it need to be something specific? Can't I just want to have a nice chat with the sister I haven't seen in years?

ANGELA. You could. But I know you too well so I'm sure there's something on your mind.

JUNIOR. Okay, okay. Guilty as charged. There is something I want to talk to you about.

ANGELA. Get to it.

JUNIOR. I just want you to be aware of what's going on around here. I don't want you to get blindsided. Just so you know…Dad is not in the best of shape.

ANGELA. He never was.

JUNIOR. It's worse. He's been extremely on edge. He's been drinking a lot more than usual and eating a lot more than usual. All he needs to do is take up smoking and he'll have the trifecta.

ANGELA. That's it?

JUNIOR. I just wanted you to know in case things are too awkward for you around here. I'm sure you don't need the stress after everything. And –

ANGELA. I'll be fine.

JUNIOR. And if it does turn out to be too much, you're welcome to stay with us. We'd love it. The girls would love to see you and have you around for a bit.

ANGELA. I'll stay here.

JUNIOR. There's no need. Dad will understand. Just tell him you want to spend some time with your nieces. Margaret is getting so big. She actually looks like you a little.

ANGELA. I know. I saw the photo of you and your whole family in today's paper.

JUNIOR. That's great that you got to see that. Do you remember Joe Davidson? It doesn't matter. Anyway he writes for *Newsday* and he got that pushed through for me. Did you read it?

ANGELA. Yes I did. Are we through?

JUNIOR. Sure. But did you read the whole article? Pretty cool, right? Things are actually changing around here for the better. The demographics of the neighborhood are changing. There are more minorities now and... let's just say you picked a good time to come home.

ANGELA. I know. I read it. I get it. There are more Democrats now, more votes for you and if you win you'll be the first Democrat in this district since the Depression. Blah, blah, blah...

JUNIOR. And I'll be the youngest ever, too.

ANGELA. Are we done?

JUNIOR. Okay, okay. You're obviously not in the mood to talk.

ANGELA. What tipped you off?

JUNIOR. I apologize. I'm just excited to see you and I wanted a talk and a beer.

ANGELA. Really? You didn't want to talk to me about running for your assembly seat?

JUNIOR. What?

ANGELA. You suggested it in that article, didn't you?

JUNIOR. No, I didn't.

ANGELA. You said that if you win, your assembly seat would be open and you'd hate to see it fall into someone else's hands.

JUNIOR. I meant a Republican.

ANGELA. Yet you mentioned that it's been in our family for thirty years.

JUNIOR. So what? It has been, right?

ANGELA. After you said it, you must have mentioned my name ten times.

JUNIOR. You're reading way too much into this.

ANGELA. You were clearly hinting at a run from someone

in the family and I know you couldn't have meant Dad or Marie.

JUNIOR. Relax. That wasn't what I was saying.

ANGELA. You suggested as much in your letters to me so don't insult my intelligence.

JUNIOR. You got my letters?

ANGELA. I got everyone's letters and calls and emails.

JUNIOR. And I guess you just didn't feel like responding?

ANGELA. Dad got my postcards. Where's Marie?

JUNIOR. Out partying.

ANGELA. That's what I should be doing.

JUNIOR. Wait. I want to settle this.

ANGELA. I have to get changed and go. So you have until I finish changing. Turn around and start talking.

(He does. As he says the following, she changes into a sexier top and starts doing her makeup.)

JUNIOR. Okay, listen. You are making an A to Z jump with this. In the interview I wasn't trying to bring up you running for office. I was just talking about you because I wanted to say how proud I was of you. And in the letters, I only mentioned the possibility of you running because I knew it was something that you planned to do before you left. I thought maybe you could use a distraction when you got home. I thought maybe with everything you've been through, that you would want to get involved and I thought I could help you. But I never heard from you so I had no idea what was going on. I figured it was a dead issue. I had no intention of talking to you about running for office.

ANGELA. And you had no ulterior motives here?

JUNIOR. Of course not.

ANGELA. You weren't hoping to get me to campaign with you and endorse you?

JUNIOR. Absolutely not. The bottom line is that I really respect and admire what you did. You served our country honorably and made us all proud.

ANGELA. I know. I read that talking point in your little flyer.

(She pulls a flyer out of her bag and tosses it on the table.)

You can turn around now.

JUNIOR. Okay. Great. So why am I getting all this attitude?

ANGELA. So you know this is going to be a tough race and you think having a little sister who's a returning vet will put you over the top, right?

JUNIOR. You think I just want you home to boost my votes?

ANGELA. This all looks great for you. Play on our family name, my service and push us both into office. Just like you used Mom's death to push yourself into the assembly seat.

JUNIOR. Whoa, whoa, whoa. I was running before she ever got sick so I don't want to hear that.

ANGELA. Okay, okay. You're right. I shouldn't have said that. I apologize.

JUNIOR. And I don't want you home just to boost my votes.

ANGELA. I'm not apologizing for that one.

JUNIOR. You really believe that?

ANGELA. Convince me I'm wrong.

JUNIOR. Of course you're wrong. You're my sister! Of course I just want you home, and I want you safe. And…you know what, I'm sorry. You don't need this shit. I'm sorry.

ANGELA. Don't give me any sympathy. Say what you were going to say.

JUNIOR. I was going to say that I was sorry for mentioning you in the flyer.

ANGELA. Sure you were.

JUNIOR. Okay, okay. You got me. I admit I did think you'd want to get involved with what I'm doing.

ANGELA. Are you referring to your promise to fight for military issues?

JUNIOR. Yes. I –

ANGELA. You don't need to go into it. Remember, I read the flyer.

JUNIOR. But the flyer doesn't go into specifics. I want to get better pay, better healthcare, and better benefits for all of you. And I want to bring attention to the issues women have to deal with over there. Too many people think that because women technically don't serve in combat that their service is somehow less honorable. The enemy doesn't care whether you're in combat or not. They'll take you out at any time, and I know you know about that. So I want to bring that issue to light. And I also wanted to bring all the sexual assault issues to light that servicewomen deal with, and I thought that this would be something that would interest you.

ANGELA. I was never sexually assaulted.

JUNIOR. I know. Forget it. It was presumptuous of me to assume you'd want to be involved. I just wanted to do something good for you and all the others. I apologize. But it wasn't about votes. It's something I really care about.

(**ANGELA** *makes some final adjustments to herself and gets in* **JUNIOR***'s face.*)

ANGELA. Listen to me and listen to me good. I am not interested in going into or getting involved in politics. I am not you. I am not Mom. Keep your phony policies and your talk of change away from me. It insults my intelligence. Do not use my name in your campaign ever again. I don't endorse it. I don't want you on tv or radio saying anything else about your "hero" sister. And don't feel too bad about this. I haven't jumped on the other side either. They're a bunch of hypocrites too.

(**JUNIOR** *and* **ANGELA** *don't notice but* **SENIOR** *enters the room.*)

CARLO SR. Who's fucking who's selves?

(JUNIOR and ANGELA back away from each other and break the tension.)

(SENIOR smiles at ANGELA.)

Look at you! You're finally home. I'm so glad I get to see you.

(He walks over to her and hugs her. JUNIOR retreats to get his beer. He chugs it in the b.g.)

(ANGELA sheepishly hugs back.)

You look beautiful, sweetheart. Let's have a drink!

(He lets the hug go and goes for the whiskey.)

ANGELA. Let's do it tomorrow. I have to run.

CARLO SR. Where are you going?

ANGELA. I'm heading down to the Shamrock to see Hutch.

CARLO SR. You go do that. Have fun and we'll talk tomorrow. We have a lot to talk about, don't we? Love you, honey.

(He kisses her on the cheek.)

CARLO SR. Carlo, give her a ride.

JUNIOR. Dad, I –

ANGELA. I'll walk.

CARLO SR. Okay. Be careful.

ANGELA. I survived the streets of Iraq. I think I can handle the streets of Hicksville.

CARLO SR. Okay, honey. Be safe and have fun. Love you.

(She leaves without exchanging a glance with JUNIOR. The door slams behind her.)

(SENIOR pours himself a whiskey. He looks at JUNIOR while he does it, as if daring JUNIOR to stop him.)

Didn't I tell you not to be here when I got back up?

JUNIOR. Don't you even start with me. You don't have any idea what just happened.

CARLO SR. Did you see what I just did? "Yes, honey." "Have fun." "See you tomorrow." That's how it's done.

JUNIOR. I was beyond nice. She's not well.

CARLO SR. Next time listen to me. I should've been the one to greet her.

JUNIOR. Dad, she was hiding in the yard waiting for you to go to bed. I saw her when I was coming up the walkway. Why do you think I came in the front?

CARLO SR. Really?

JUNIOR. Yes, really.

CARLO SR. So you saw her hiding from me and thought that meant she wanted to talk to you?

JUNIOR. She deserved to be greeted by a coherent and sober family member. Marie's wherever the hell she is and you…you're you and…the hell with it. I'm not going to bother. I'm leaving.

CARLO SR. You're going to have a drink with me and a little chat.

JUNIOR. Now you want me to stay?

(**SENIOR** *pours another whiskey. He puts it in front of* **JUNIOR**.)

CARLO SR. Sit.

JUNIOR. I've already had a beer and I have to drive.

CARLO SR. Don't worry. I heard that this stuff is watered down.

(**SENIOR** *smiles at* **JUNIOR**.)

(*The lights go down.*)

Scene II

(The kitchen is only lit by the light above the stove. We hear voices coming from offstage.)

(BANG! **ANGELA**'s *back slams into the kitchen door. She is immediately followed by* **HUTCH**. *He kisses her up against the door.)*

ANGELA. *(offstage)* Calm down. Let me get the door open.

HUTCH. *(offstage)* You mean we have to go inside?

(She opens the door and they spill into the kitchen, leaving the door open.)

*(***HUTCH*** grabs at her butt.)*

Wow. The army really did great things for your ass.

(He smacks it.)

ANGELA. You haven't lost your way with words.

(She kisses him and takes him down on the table.)

HUTCH. I'm not kidding. I just want to –

ANGELA. I bet you would.

(She kisses him. They make out some more. He puts his hand up her shirt.)

(She stops him.)

ANGELA. Let's cool it for a minute.

HUTCH. Are you serious?

ANGELA. Relax, I'm not teasing you. I want another drink and then we can head upstairs.

(She gets off of him. She turns the lights on and grabs some glasses and looks through the cabinets.)

(He stays on the table, sprawled out, looking like he's just passed out.)

Did I wipe you out already?

HUTCH. Fuck no! Are we going up to your room?

ANGELA. It'll be a nice nostalgia trip.

HUTCH. How do you mean?

ANGELA. Figures you wouldn't remember.

HUTCH. You weren't my first.

ANGELA. I didn't say I was. It was OUR first time.

HUTCH. Oh yes. And we had to be really quiet so we wouldn't wake up your parents.

ANGELA. This time we just have to worry about my dad.

HUTCH. That's good. Dads never hear anything. Mothers are always the ones with the good hearing. They have like sonar in their heads or something.

ANGELA. Oh yeah. And my mom was as good as they come. She could hear us doing it at your house.

HUTCH. Yeah. I'm sorry about her by the way.

ANGELA. It was a long time ago, Hutch.

HUTCH. I know and I'm sorry. I never even sent you a card.

ANGELA. Cards are bullshit.

(She hands him a glass of whiskey, but he pours most of his into her glass, leaving just a drop in his.)

Why aren't you drinking?

HUTCH. I have to perform in a few minutes.

ANGELA. So what? So do I.

HUTCH. You're a girl. You can just lay there.

ANGELA. Fuck you.

HUTCH. That's the idea.

(He grabs her and starts kissing her. She accepts the kiss but doesn't let it go further, stopping him again.)

ANGELA. What's your rush?

HUTCH. It's getting late.

ANGELA. It's getting early, actually.

(She goes to take a sip of her drink, but he grabs her hand and stops her.)

HUTCH. Wait. Wait. A toast to you being home.

(He goes to clink glasses. She stops.)

ANGELA. Wait, wait. And a toast to you, me, and hopefully Marie leaving this place behind.

(She goes to clink glasses but he stops.)

HUTCH. I haven't agreed to go anywhere yet. Especially since you haven't told me where we're supposed to go.

ANGELA. What does it matter?

HUTCH. Of course it matters.

ANGELA. We're going somewhere nicer.

HUTCH. Like Levittown?

ANGELA. I'm serious.

HUTCH. Me, too. I'm not saying I won't go, but I want to know where we're going.

ANGELA. No matter where, it's better for you than this place. You're a bartender at a townie bar with no college degree, no girlfriend. You live with your parents. You do nothing but drink, eat, play softball and hockey, and bet on football on Sunday.

HUTCH. I didn't realize my life was that awesome.

(She gives him a dirty look.)

I'm kidding, I'm kidding. But come on, my whole family is here.

ANGELA. You don't even like them.

HUTCH. That's a very good point.

ANGELA. Say yes.

HUTCH. No.

ANGELA. No?

HUTCH. No, no. Not no as in, "I'm not going." I'm just saying no to saying yes at the moment. Wait. I'm getting confused. If I don't say yes to you right now does that mean we're not going to have sex?

ANGELA. No.

HUTCH. No we're not going to have sex or no it –

ANGELA. Will you shut up and listen to me?

HUTCH. I am. I want to know where we're going.

ANGELA. I want you to admit that anything's better than this. There's nothing but losers around here. And the worst part is that they think they're winners and "patriotic Americans" just because they kiss the ass of people like my dad and me. Did you notice the way they were fawning all over me at the bar? How patronizing.

HUTCH. You don't know the half of it. Wait till you go to an Islanders or Mets game and see what they do there.

ANGELA. What do they do?

HUTCH. Every game, they put a returning veteran on the big screen and everyone gives them a standing ovation while they play that "Proud to be an American" song. And then the crowd inevitably chants, "U.S.A."

ANGELA. Of course. Doing their part for the war effort. Where would we be without them?

HUTCH. Wow.

ANGELA. Wow, what?

HUTCH. I'm still surprised to hear you talk like this.

ANGELA. Even with everything we spoke about in the past few months?

HUTCH. I thought maybe you were just going through a phase and then when you got home you'd –

ANGELA. I'd what? Run for office and have my face plastered on a poster right next to my brother?

HUTCH. That was your plan back in the day.

ANGELA. That was a long time ago.

HUTCH. It seems like yesterday to me.

ANGELA. Of course it does. You're in the same exact place I left you so the days just kind of blend for you.

HUTCH. Ohhh. That was a hit below the belt.

ANGELA. Stop it. I'm teasing you.

(She takes his hand.)

ANGELA. You know I thought about you a lot over there.

HUTCH. What did you think about me? Did you think about how you left this handsome, intelligent, strapping young man at home?

ANGELA. I thought about how you were the only one who tried to talk me out of going. I thought about how I wish I had listened to you, about how maybe I should've taken your call more seriously.

HUTCH. But you didn't.

ANGELA. I know.

HUTCH. Maybe it's all for the best.

ANGELA. Maybe.

(She kisses him. He breaks it.)

HUTCH. Can I ask you something?

ANGELA. Of course you can.

HUTCH. Is all that stuff I heard true?

ANGELA. What stuff?

HUTCH. About what happened over there, to you?

ANGELA. It depends. What did you hear?

HUTCH. I heard that you met a guy, and you were engaged, and that you both were involved in an ambush, and….

ANGELA. Say it.

HUTCH. He was killed. Was all of that right?

ANGELA. We weren't in the same ambush.

(She breaks away from him and goes to refill her drink.)

HUTCH. I'm sorry. I shouldn't have brought it up.

ANGELA. It would've come up eventually.

HUTCH. So is that over?

ANGELA. He's dead!

HUTCH. You know what I mean.

ANGELA. It's as over as it will ever be.

HUTCH. What about you?

ANGELA. What about me?

HUTCH. Are you okay and…I don't even know what I'm saying. Forget it. I'm no good at these kinds of conversations.

(He attacks her and starts kissing her.)

(She laughs and obliges. He takes her down on the table and they go at it during the following exchange.)

ANGELA. So you're going to come with me?

(He starts to unbutton her shirt again but she stops him.)

HUTCH. Yeah. Let's go right now.

ANGELA. Are you listening to me?

(He starts to unzip her pants.)

Hutch, I want an answer.

(She stops him.)

Goddamnit!

(She gets out from under him, grabs his arm, twists it around and puts him face down onto the table in a hammerlock.)

*(**HUTCH** gives a little yell from the pain, but he also laughs through it.)*

HUTCH. Holy shit! Ease up, ease up.

ANGELA. Stop whining I'm not even applying full pressure.

HUTCH. I'm actually kind of into this, you know that, right?

ANGELA. Listen to me, Jonathan Hutchinson, I am getting you out of here before you become one of them!

HUTCH. It'll never happen.

ANGELA. I'm surprised it hasn't already.

HUTCH. I'm too good.

ANGELA. It's only a matter of time until you meet a girl who makes you settle down and raise your kids their way.

HUTCH. I hope she's hot.

(She tightens the grip.)

HUTCH. Ow, ow, ow. Fuck!!! Okay. I'll think long and hard about coming with you.

ANGELA. How hard?

HUTCH. As hard as I was before you put me in this hold.

(She gives one last twist on his shoulder before she lets him go.)

(He rubs his shoulder.)

HUTCH. *(cont.)* Fuck!

ANGELA. You know what I don't understand about you?

HUTCH. How I turned into such a pussy?

ANGELA. How you can stand living here with all of them. They all pretend to believe in all this bullshit and then they call you a loser for speaking the truth.

HUTCH. I get to play the bad guy, like Roddy Piper. I'm a heel.

ANGELA. They're the heels.

HUTCH. And I tried to tell you that years ago. But you had to go serve your country. Just like the rest of your family, waving your little flags.

ANGELA. I've learned.

HUTCH. Have you? Or will you soon be going back to who you were? And as I recall, who you "were" thought I was not good enough.

ANGELA. Did you read all the stuff I wrote to you?

HUTCH. Every word.

ANGELA. So you know that I now see everything you used to talk about, all of the hypocrisies and all of the lies.

HUTCH. All of them?

ANGELA. All. There's no going back for me.

HUTCH. You know it's a shame you had to go through all that shit just to learn something that you could've figured out with eight minutes of rational thought.

(She walks away from him.)

ANGELA. Get out of here now.

(He runs over to her.)

HUTCH. I'm sorry. I didn't mean that. I just really missed you, and I wish you never left, and I wish you never put yourself through all that shit.

(He pulls her close and kisses her.)

(She caresses his face a bit.)

ANGELA. Those days are over. Now we're going to get out of here.

HUTCH. Right now?

ANGELA. We're leaving all of this behind. All the bullshit.

HUTCH. Awesome.

(He gets a little closer to her. He grabs her hands and stands her up, holds her body to his. He kisses her. She gets into it and kisses back. She separates.)

(He picks her up and she monkey hugs him as she kisses him. He carries her out of the kitchen towards the living room, but they bump into the fridge.)

(That breaks them up and they laugh.)

ANGELA. Shh. We're going to wake my dad.

HUTCH. Don't worry, he's down.

(She laughs. They kiss again as he carries her off stage this time.)

(The lights go down.)

Scene III

(The morning light shines through the kitchen windows as the lights come up.)

*(**CARLO SR.**, wearing pajamas and a bathrobe, finishes making breakfast. He looks out the window. He hurries as if he sees someone coming.)*

(He takes the plate of eggs and toast and puts it on the table next to another one.)

(There are two breakfast settings ready.)

(He walks over to the back door and looks out.)

(He comes back in and closes the door.)

(He grabs the bottle of whiskey out of the cabinet.)

*(As he's doing it, **MARIE** enters through the back door. She's dressed like she just came home from a club, miniskirt, skimpy top and heels.)*

*(She sees **CARLO** and immediately comes to a stop.)*

MARIE. Daddy, what are you doing up?

CARLO SR. I could ask you the same question.

MARIE. I'm sure you will.

(He pours some whiskey into his coffee.)

MARIE. I see we're medicating.

CARLO SR. Not we. Just me. Unless…

(He offers some.)

MARIE. It's seven thirty in the morning.

CARLO SR. It is. Why are you getting in so late? Or early I should say?

(He pours more whiskey into this cup.)

MARIE. We hit an after hours place and had to wait pretty long for a train, and then we passed out and wound up in Ronkonkoma and…would you stop that?

(She comes over and takes the whiskey from him and puts it on the counter.)

CARLO SR. Excuse me! I can smell the liquor on your breath, too.

MARIE. I don't drink with breakfast.

CARLO SR. You're missing out.

MARIE. Where's Angie?

CARLO SR. What are you wearing?

MARIE. Very little.

CARLO SR. So I see. And apparently all of New York City did too.

MARIE. Is she upstairs?

CARLO SR. How about leaving a little to the imagination next time?

MARIE. That's it. I'm going up to see her.

(She starts for the door.)

CARLO SR. You don't even know if she's here.

MARIE. Is she?

CARLO SR. She rolled in pretty late.

MARIE. Okay. Great.

(She moves to the door again.)

CARLO SR. Wait, wait. Let's eat.

MARIE. I want to see her before I pass out.

CARLO SR. But I want you to have breakfast with me.

MARIE. Why are you acting so weird?

CARLO SR. I want to have breakfast with you. How is that weird?

MARIE. Have you spoken to her?

CARLO SR. A little. And now I want to speak with you.

MARIE. But I'm about to go from drunk to hungover.

CARLO SR. No buts, and cover yours with this.

(He takes off his robe and gives it to her.)

MARIE. You're so ridiculous.

CARLO SR. You're an adult, you can wear what you want but I don't like seeing you in it. Now put it on. I used those organic eggs you wanted me to try. We're eating healthy!

(She relents, puts on the robe, and takes a seat at the table.)

MARIE. Organic eggs and whiskey?

CARLO SR. Do they make organic whiskey?

(MARIE jumps up from her seat as if something just shocked her.)

MARIE. Oh my God! I am so, so sorry! Happy birthday!

(She hugs him.)

I haven't gone to bed yet so for me it's still yesterday. I'm sorry. I really didn't forget.

CARLO SR. I really did. Don't worry about it.

MARIE. I should've been the one to make you breakfast. I'll tell you what, I'll make dinner tonight. Now that Angie is here, we can have Carlo and Tara and the girls over and do a whole family dinner tonight and I'll cook everything! But I have to get some rest.

(She kisses him on the head and starts for the door.)

CARLO SR. Whoa, whoa. Slow down.

MARIE. But if I'm going to make dinner I need to sleep.

CARLO SR. You're not going to make dinner. We're not having anyone over here tonight. Now finish your breakfast.

MARIE. Why wouldn't we have dinner? It's your birthday and Angie's home. We have two reasons to celebrate.

CARLO SR. Turning sixty-one is nothing to celebrate and I'm not sure Angie's homecoming is either. Now sit and eat.

(MARIE sighs, relents, and sits.)

MARIE. What's going on?

CARLO SR. Did you speak to your brother?

MARIE. Yes, I start everyday by checking in with Carlo at the asscrack of dawn.

CARLO SR. You can knock off the sarcasm.

MARIE. And you can tell me what's going on.

CARLO SR. Let's just say that things are going to be a little different with Angie.

MARIE. I know. She told me...I mean you already told –

CARLO SR. Whoa. What was that?

MARIE. I was saying that you –

CARLO SR. You said, "She told me."

MARIE. Will you let me finish? You –

CARLO SR. Has she called you?

MARIE. No. You told –

CARLO SR. Then why did you say that she "told" you?

MARIE. Jesus Christ! Let me finish. I meant to say that you told me already that things were going to be different.

CARLO SR. You started to say that she –

MARIE. Holy shit! I know. I'm out of it and I misspoke. All I know is what you said she said in the postcards.

CARLO SR. Which is nothing.

MARIE. Exactly. I know nothing. I have to go to bed.

CARLO SR. We're not done.

MARIE. I am. I'm now officially hungover.

CARLO SR. *(hands her his whiskey laced coffee)* Here. It's a good hangover cure.

MARIE. More alcohol?

CARLO SR. Works every time. Now what were you saying?

MARIE. Nothing. I don't know. Can I go to bed now?

CARLO SR. Eat a little first.

(She rolls her eyes, but finally eats some eggs.)

I need to remind you that she just came home from a pretty tough place, so I think we all need to have a little patience.

MARIE. So is that it? You needed this whole production just to tell me to be patient with her?

CARLO SR. You just need to know that we can't expect her to just jump right back into who she was before. She been through hell and she's behaving...as expected in a way.

MARIE. These eggs suck.

(She spits them out.)

CARLO SR. Are you listening to me?

MARIE. Yes. Can I go to bed now?

CARLO SR. So I can count on you to not add any drama?

MARIE. Yes.

CARLO SR. You'll be my partner?

MARIE. Is that all?

CARLO SR. You don't have anymore of those skirts, do you?

MARIE. Yes. Anything else?

CARLO SR. I'm thinking that we should do this more often.

MARIE. Drink together?

CARLO SR. Eat breakfast. You're usually rolling in as I'm waking up.

MARIE. You know how much weight I'll gain if I keep eating right before I go to bed?

CARLO SR. Yeah. You won't be able to dress like a hooker anymore.

MARIE. Daddy!

CARLO SR. I'm teasing. There are plenty of fat hookers.

MARIE. Dad!

CARLO SR. I'm sorry. I'm joking. So what's going on with you?

MARIE. I'm hungover.

CARLO SR. No. I mean do you have a boyfriend? Do people your age even have boyfriends anymore? Do...

*(We hear **HUTCH** singing offstage.)*

MARIE. What is that?

CARLO SR. Oh, Christ. It's our surprise guest for the morning.

*(**HUTCH**, wearing just his boxers, enters the kitchen.)*

HUTCH. Look at this! A family breakfast! When was the last time I was at one of these? Marie, you're looking gorgeous.

(He kisses her on the cheek.)

CARLO SR. Where are your pants?

HUTCH. I don't see you in years and that's the greeting I get?

CARLO SR. I don't appreciate the chorus of moans I heard all night from the two of you.

*(***HUTCH*** laughs.)*

MARIE. I really didn't need to hear that.

HUTCH. Wow. You could hear us?

*(***CARLO SR.*** pulls the bath robe off of* **MARIE** *and tosses it at* **HUTCH.***)*

CARLO SR. Put it on now.

HUTCH. No problem.

(while putting the robe on)

Mr. C, I feel so close to you in this.

*(***HUTCH*** helps himself to a bowl of cereal.)*

CARLO SR. Did I say you could eat?

HUTCH. So…Angie's gone bat-shit crazy, huh?

CARLO SR. I see you're handling this with your usual sensitivity.

HUTCH. I don't mean it in a bad way. She's just a little screwy.

CARLO SR. Maybe there's a reason for it, asshole. Unlike you she tried to do something with her life. I'm sure she'd be nice and happy if she hung out at the bar with you all the time.

HUTCH. Which is exactly what I advised her to do way back when. And think about how much happier we'd all be if she'd listened.

*(***HUTCH*** takes a seat at the table.)*

So, Marie, Marie…

MARIE. What? What?

HUTCH. What do you think about what's going on?

MARIE. It's family business, so stay out of it.

HUTCH. No, no. I mean are you going with her or not?

MARIE. I don't know what you're talking about.

HUTCH. Bullshit.

MARIE. I don't. Now shut up.

CARLO SR. What are you talking about?

HUTCH. Angie's plans for the future. She wants me and Marie to come live with –

MARIE. Shut the fuck up, Hutch!

HUTCH. Is she serious or has she completely flipped her lid?

MARIE. Asshole.

CARLO SR. What's going on?

MARIE. Nothing.

HUTCH. Angie wants –

MARIE. Shut the fuck up!

*(**MARIE** gets up and throws a piece of toast at **HUTCH**. **CARLO** grabs her and sits her back down.)*

HUTCH. Nice skirt.

CARLO SR. Marie, what's going on?

MARIE. Angie'll tell you.

HUTCH. She wants –

MARIE. I said she'll tell him!

CARLO SR. How do you know about all this?

*(**MARIE** doesn't repsond. She just gives **HUTCH** a dirty look.)*

Marie!

MARIE. We've been talking.

CARLO SR. What do you mean?

MARIE. What do you think?

CARLO SR. I thought she was ignoring everybody.

MARIE. Not me.

HUTCH. Me either. Just you and Carlo.

CARLO SR. So she did call you?

MARIE. Yes.

CARLO SR. How could you not tell me about this?

MARIE. She asked me to keep it private.

CARLO SR. So she doesn't return anyone's calls but yours…

HUTCH. And mine.

CARLO SR. And you didn't think you should tell me this? You knew how concerned I was.

MARIE. You knew she was alive and well.

CARLO SR. I knew she was alive.

MARIE. And she said she was going to come home and talk to you so I didn't see it as a big deal.

CARLO SR. You didn't think that maybe I might have a better idea about what she's going through and that I should be involved?

HUTCH. Did you blow a gasket too when you got back from Vietnam?

CARLO SR. Get out of here before I –

HUTCH. Oh please. The only thing that you could frighten is an all- you-can-eat buffet.

CARLO SR. Get out.

(**CARLO** *charges at* **HUTCH**. **HUTCH** *laughs while he runs away from* **CARLO**, *only making him angrier.*)

MARIE. Dad!

(**MARIE** *steps between them stopping the craziness.* **HUTCH** *just smiles at* **CARLO**.)

(**ANGIE**, *wearing her pajamas, enters the kitchen, looking a little beat and hung over.*)

ANGELA. Okay! Everyone calm down!

MARIE. Angie!

(**MARIE** *runs over and hugs* **ANGIE**.)

HUTCH. This is so nice. I'm so glad I'm here for this family reunion.

MARIE. Angie, I didn't tell him anything.

ANGELA. It's okay. We're going to talk right now.

CARLO SR. Yes, we are. Everybody out.

HUTCH. I want to stay for this.

MARIE. Me, too.

CARLO SR. Marie, take the boy home.

MARIE. He can walk.

CARLO SR. Now.

ANGELA. It's okay, Marie. We'll talk later.

HUTCH. What about me?

ANGELA. I'll call you.

HUTCH. Okay. Can the boy take his cereal?

(CARLO picks up the cereal and puts it on the counter, nudging HUTCH towards the door.)

CARLO SR. Take him out the front and don't interrupt us.

MARIE. Okay, okay. Let's go.

(HUTCH kisses ANGELA and smacks her ass.)

HUTCH. Talk to you later. Good time last night. Bye, Mr Colletti.

MARIE. Move it along, asshole.

HUTCH. I'm coming.

(They leave the room.)

(ANGELA looks up at CARLO SR.)

ANGELA. Happy birthday.

CARLO SR. Thank you.

ANGELA. Okay. So…what's up?

CARLO SR. Why don't you tell me?

ANGELA. Are you mad at me?

CARLO SR. Why would I be?

ANGELA. Let's not play this game. You know what I'm talking about.

CARLO SR. Fine. And no, I'm not mad. If that's how you felt you needed to handle things, I can understand that, and I can probably understand what you're feeling.

But if you were talking to Marie all this time, why wouldn't you at least have her tell us you were okay? Why have her pretend that you were ignoring her too?

ANGELA. What did it matter? I sent you some postcards.

CARLO SR. You sent me two and all they had was your name on it.

ANGELA. I just wanted you to know I was alive.

CARLO SR. Mission accomplished then. So...you know what, forget it. It doesn't matter. I'm just glad you're home. So now, please tell me what the hell's going on.

ANGELA. What do you know already?

CARLO SR. Just let me hear it from you.

ANGELA. Okay. In a nutshell, I have purchased some land in Colorado, in the middle of nowhere. Everything I'll need is within reach. I'm building a little cabin there. I'm home to pick up Hutch and Marie and take them to live with me out there. You are welcome to come too.

CARLO SR. You, me, Hutch and Marie living in the mountains? What are we, Swiss Family Robinson?

ANGELA. If you don't want to come, don't, but don't make fun of me.

CARLO SR. I'm not. I'm worried.

ANGELA. If there was a time to worry it was while I was over there.

CARLO SR. I worried plenty and I worried again when you were discharged and didn't come straight home. What have you been doing with yourself? Just hiding in Colorado?

ANGELA. I travelled around.

CARLO SR. Yeah, I noticed the postmarks.

ANGELA. Then why did you ask?

CARLO SR. I don't know. I don't know what I'm saying.

ANGELA. Are we done?

CARLO SR. No, we're not done.

ANGELA. What else?

CARLO SR. What else? How about your plan to lead us all into the wilderness?

ANGELA. What about it?

CARLO SR. You're suggesting we unplug from our lives and go live in the middle of nowhere in Colorado? Are we becoming Amish?

ANGELA. Stop making jokes.

CARLO SR. You really think you can convince everyone to do this? What about Carlo?

ANGELA. I'm not asking him.

CARLO SR. Is this all because of his flyer and the interview and all that? Because that was all a misunderstanding. He would never do anything deliberately to hurt or use you.

ANGELA. I've never seen a politician, Democrat or Republican, who doesn't use soldiers every chance they get.

CARLO SR. Yes. Many do. But Carlo is different and you know that.

ANGELA. Why? Because he's your son and my brother?

CARLO SR. He's a good guy. He's trying to do some good.

ANGELA. You just say that because he's your son. The bottom line is that the world is a sick place because of people like Carlo.

CARLO SR. He's your brother!

ANGELA. That's the best argument you have?

CARLO SR. Okay, calm down. You just got back from a rough place and you saw a lot of stuff. It warps your mind for a little bit. When I got back from Vietnam I did the same thing as you, and I wandered the country for six months and contemplated all kinds of crazy things. But then I cooled off and realized that everything was okay and it was time to start my life. So listen, you don't –

ANGELA. "I don't know what I'm saying and this all will fade." Is that where you were going to go with that?

(She sits at the table and picks at what's left of **MARIE***'s breakfast.)*

CARLO SR. I know it's hard for you to see right now, but your thoughts are completely irrational.

ANGELA. Mine are?

CARLO SR. You're saying that your brother is one of the reasons the world is sick.

ANGELA. I'm not giving him that much credit. I said people like him.

CARLO SR. Holy shit! Wow. I'm at a loss right now.

ANGELA. Are we done?

CARLO SR. No! Are you going to bring this attitude into the Christening on Sunday?

ANGELA. Are you out of your mind? I'm not going to that.

CARLO SR. I figured that's why you chose now to come home.

ANGELA. Yes. I finally decided to come home so I can watch a child molester pour water on a kid's head.

CARLO SR. You and your sister with the sarcasm.

ANGELA. These eggs suck.

(She spits them out.)

CARLO SR. Forget the goddamn eggs.

(He grabs the plate and puts it in the sink.)

So if you're not here for the Christening, how come you finally decided to come home?

ANGELA. I told you. I'm here to get Marie and Hutch.

CARLO SR. Right. To move to the log cabin.

ANGELA. To move to a place where we won't contribute to any of this anymore, any of the stuff you were raised in, any of the stuff you and Mom raised us in, and any of the stuff Carlo and Tara are raising their kids in.

CARLO SR. The stuff your mother and I raised you in? How did we get dragged into this?

ANGELA. Let's not get into it.

CARLO SR. I think I'd like to hear this.

ANGELA. I don't think you do. I think you're better off just doing what you've been doing all these years.

CARLO SR. You obviously have something to say, so just say it.

ANGELA. Okay, fine. But it's more of a question actually.

CARLO SR. Then ask it.

ANGELA. Why did you let Mom baptize us and raise us Catholic?

CARLO SR. Come again?

ANGELA. You heard me.

CARLO SR. It was important to her and she believed in it.

ANGELA. She believed in gay rights, she was pro-choice, she didn't believe the Pope was infallible, she told us that sex before marriage was okay as long as we were in love and responsible, she taught us about contraception. So exactly which parts of this religion did she believe?

CARLO SR. What can I say? She's dead now and we can't ask her.

ANGELA. We don't need to. She just did what she was raised to do. She did the "right" thing. Society teaches us that we must raise our kids in a religion. Those who don't, are freaks. So she went along with it and so did you.

CARLO SR. She probably just believed in the main part. She probably just believed that Jesus was God's son and all that.

ANGELA. I think she was too intelligent to think that virgins can have babies or that people can rise from the dead.

CARLO SR. Fine. You've made your point. It's nothing new. Most people know that most people just go through the motions with religion. It's no big deal.

ANGELA. And on Sunday, Carlo and Tara are going to start the whole cycle over again with the new baby.

CARLO SR. It's their kid. I can't tell them how to raise her.

ANGELA. Like you would anyway. You know that they don't really believe in any of it. Neither do you. Neither does Marie. Why don't you try and put a stop to it?

CARLO SR. Who gives a shit? So the kid will learn about a bunch of silly fairytales, feel some shame and guilt, get over it and then she'll be like the rest of us and go through the motions with it. Cool off the crusade.

ANGELA. It's wrong. You know it.

CARLO SR. It's bullshit. Who cares?

ANGELA. I just got back from a place where I wouldn't have been if it wasn't for religion. So I don't want to hear that it's just bullshit and who cares.

CARLO SR. You're equating a baptism with those nuts over there?

ANGELA. Think about it. There isn't as much of a difference as you think.

CARLO SR. But –

ANGELA. Just think about it. Please.

CARLO SR. Okay. I tell you what. I'll think about all of that if you agree to stay here for six months –

ANGELA. No.

CARLO SR. Let me finish. You stay here for six months and see a therapist and then –

ANGELA. No.

CARLO SR. If you still feel the same way about everything after six months, I'll give you and Marie my blessing for this little adventure.

ANGELA. I don't need your blessing and Marie is an adult. She doesn't need it either.

CARLO SR. Listen, while we're here, we can work on everything together. I know what you're feeling and trust me, this will pass.

ANGELA. The phase you're referring to has passed. I got it out while I was travelling around. And what you see now is the result.

CARLO SR. And the result is that you're mad at me and your mother for raising you Catholic and mad at Carlo for raising his kids that way?

ANGELA. It's a little more complicated than that.

CARLO SR. Are you suicidal?

ANGELA. What? Where did that come from?

CARLO SR. Are you?

ANGELA. I am not suicidal. I'm not sick. I'm not crazy and I'm not suffering from any post-traumatic stress. I have just opened my eyes and I see things differently now.

CARLO SR. When I was a kid, we had this thing called the 60s, where we questioned anything and everything. So please, do us all a favor and stop acting like you're breaking new ground here. These are all questions that have been dealt with before.

ANGELA. That's right. But nothing changes.

CARLO SR. What are you talking about? Things have changed.

ANGELA. Just the styles.

CARLO SR. You are twenty-nine years old. What do you know about change?

ANGELA. I know that people are still fighting for the same things they fought for years ago, money, religion, oil, land, power, whatever. I know that we're still fighting just like your father fought against the Japanese, and you fought against the Viet Cong, and I fought against the Arabs, and I'm sure at least one of your grandkids will fight against somebody one day, too. That doesn't sound like a lot of change to me.

CARLO SR. What? How did we get onto this? I thought we were talking about religion.

ANGELA. We are. Now let me ask you a question, do you love your country?

CARLO SR. Are you serious?

ANGELA. Answer the fucking question?

CARLO SR. Of course I love my country.

ANGELA. Great. Now what does it mean to love your country? Does that mean you love the actual land? The people? The constitution? The flag? The government? What if you don't like Wyoming or Alabama or the Dakotas? Does that mean you don't love America?

CARLO SR. Honey, you are over thinking this one–big time.

ANGELA. You don't even know what it means to love your country. You just say that you love your country because it's the right thing to say.

CARLO SR. Get the hell out of here with that. I do love my country. I put my life on the line for it.

ANGELA. I know. So did I.

CARLO SR. So then what the hell are we arguing about? We both love our country.

ANGELA. No! We don't love it. We worship it. Well, you do. I did.

CARLO SR. Worship it?

ANGELA. See you may not go to church and kneel for a prayer or genuflect in front of the crucifix, but no matter what wrong your country does you'll stand for that anthem and recite that pledge of allegiance. Because that is your religion. And that's the one you raised us in. Mom did the Catholic thing, you did the America thing. One way or another, we were taught to follow orders from some pretty high authorities, weren't we? If we question the church, we're blasphemers. If we question our country, we're traitors. Either way, you guys raised us to follow orders, didn't you?

CARLO SR. Bullshit. I did teach you to question your government, so don't hand me that crap.

ANGELA. Please. You taught us that we "could," but it was very clear that at the end of the day, the right thing to do was to back your country, no matter what. You raised us with that super-patriotism.

CARLO SR. No, I raised you to be patriotic but I didn't raise you to be like the shit-kicking lunatics in the Midwest.

ANGELA. There isn't as much of a difference between us and them as you think. Doing anything in the name of patriotism justifies anything in the name of patriotism, no?

CARLO SR. Honey, you've gone off the deep end on this one. You have gone through some awful things and of course you are going to have some resentment towards your country. You will not hate it for long. I once felt everything you're feeling. And, yes, I even hated my country for a bit. But –

ANGELA. I'm sure all of these thoughts occurred to you when you were young, but you didn't have the balls to express them. It was much easier to step in line and raise us the "right" way. And because of that, I enlisted, almost died, and lost someone I loved.

CARLO SR. I never thought that would happen. They don't send women into combat. What happened to you was a fluke.

ANGELA. So if I were a boy, would you have tried to stop me from enlisting?

CARLO SR. I don't know.

ANGELA. You never even thought about it, did you? Why bother? You know the right thing to do is to send your kids off to fight, right?

CARLO SR. We've all thought about those things. Just because we didn't come to the same conclusion as you doesn't mean we didn't think about it. It's the same fight, generation after generation and –

ANGELA. But nothing changes. Keep perpetuating the cycle.

CARLO SR. Things are what they are and if what you're saying was really the solution, we would've tried it a long time ago.

ANGELA. Things are what they are because we keep them that way, because no one has the balls to change it, because they're too afraid to be called crazy, or a traitor, or a lunatic.

CARLO SR. So you're going to change the world?

ANGELA. I wish I could, but there are too many people like Carlo who will raise their kids just like you and Mom did. Your parents raised you one way, you and Mom raised us the same way, and Carlo is continuing the tradition. So is everyone else in America. And people wonder why nothing changes.

(He walks away from her, without looking at her, heading to the liquor cabinet.)

I warned you not to get into it. It's a lot for you to process right now. It sucks to have everything you believe exposed as a fraud. But you'll get over it.

CARLO SR. And you will get over it, too.

ANGELA. I have.

(He smiles. He grabs the whiskey and pours two glasses and hands her one.)

CARLO SR. So you really came home with a lot to settle, huh?

ANGELA. You asked. I would've just kept my mouth shut.

CARLO SR. Fair enough. And let me ask you this, how long are you sticking around?

ANGELA. Just until Saturday.

CARLO SR. So what's the plan for Marie? Is she going to meet you out there?

ANGELA. No. If she comes, she has to leave with me on Saturday.

CARLO SR. She can't. She's going to be godmother, remember?

ANGELA. She has a choice she has to make.

CARLO SR. What are you up to now?

ANGELA. Nothing.

CARLO SR. You're going to make her choose between you and Carlo?

ANGELA. That's not how I'd put it, but that is the situation.

CARLO SR. So if she sticks around for the Christening on Sunday, you won't let her come out there next week?

ANGELA. That's right.

CARLO SR. So you did come home for the Christening, didn't you?

ANGELA. I guess in a manner of speaking.

(**JUNIOR** *comes through the back door carrying two posters in his hand.*)

JUNIOR. What is your problem?

CARLO SR. Carlo, this is not a good time.

JUNIOR. Why don't you ask her what she did last night?

CARLO SR. Go home and I'll call you later.

JUNIOR. Whose handiwork is this?

(*He unrolls the poster. It's one of his campaign posters. It has a big photo of* **JUNIOR** *on it, except the teeth are blacked out, a mustache is drawn on it and a bubble with the word, "Hypocrite," is above his face.*)

(**CARLO SENIOR** *takes the poster.*)

Every poster by the Shamrock is like that. And what about this one?

(*He unrolls another one. The bubble over his head on this one says "cock."*)

(**CARLO SENIOR** *takes it.*)

CARLO SR. You didn't do this, did you?

JUNIOR. It was obviously her and Hutch. Who else would do it?

ANGELA. You said the neighborhood is changing. Maybe you're not as popular as you think.

CARLO SR. Why the hell would you do this? If you don't want to help your brother out, that's one thing, but don't try and sabotage his campaign.

(**MARIE** *enters the kitchen and observes, but no one notices her.*)

JUNIOR. What is the matter with you?

ANGELA. Absolutely nothing, and if you raise your voice to me again, I'm going to give you a smack.

JUNIOR. Is that right?

(*She gets up and moves towards him.* **CARLO SENIOR** *steps in the way.*)

CARLO SR. If there's going to be any smacking, I'm going to be the one to do it.

MARIE. This is nice.

CARLO SR. Your sister and Hutch decided they'd play Picasso last night.

(He tosses the poster to her.)

MARIE. This was you? I saw one of these at 7-11!

JUNIOR. Oh great. There's more? Holy shit!

CARLO SR. Goddmanit. How many of these did you ruin?

ANGELA. You don't even know for sure that it was me.

CARLO SR. Answer me!

ANGELA. Just those and the ones at 7-11.

JUNIOR. Oh just those. Great.

CARLO SR. Carlo, why don't you go take those down?

JUNIOR. She should take them down.

CARLO SR. You leave now, take them down, and I will call you later.

JUNIOR. Fine. Whatever. Call me later.

(JUNIOR leaves, slamming the door.)

(CARLO SR. looks at the defaced poster. He shakes his head.)

CARLO SR. This is the thanks we get for spending the last few years worrying about you. Unbelievable.

(He throws the poster down in front of her.)

I think it's best if you leave sooner. Don't wait for Saturday.

ANGELA. Okay. I'll leave tomorrow.

(He gets in MARIE's face.)

CARLO SR. And as for you, young lady, you think you're slick? Watering down my whiskeys? I have a private stash somewhere else so you might as well give it up. Now I want everyone out of my kitchen in five minutes. If anyone is here when I get back down, I'm knocking heads.

(CARLO SR. storms out of the room. MARIE shakes her head and laughs.)

MARIE. You are something else.

ANGELA. What's the problem?

MARIE. Do you have to make this whole thing so difficult?

ANGELA. I'm not making anything difficult. Dad had questions and I gave him answers. It's not my fault he doesn't like them.

MARIE. *(holding up defaced poster)* And this?

ANGELA. I don't have time to sit here and defend myself. Let's just say that I had my reasons.

MARIE. You had your reasons. That's great.

ANGELA. Are you coming with me or not?

MARIE. I'd like to. I really would.

ANGELA. What's stopping you?

MARIE. Does Hutch really have to come?

ANGELA. You'll like him when you get to know him.

MARIE. Well, who's going to take care of Dad if I go?

ANGELA. He can take care of himself.

MARIE. You haven't been around, Angie. You don't know.

ANGELA. It seems to me like you do a ton of partying and not much caretaking.

MARIE. Bullshit. I'm the one who is always sneaking healthier foods in here. I water down his whiskey and yes, I even got to his secret stash that he just mentioned. It's right behind his bureau with his gun. So don't tell me.

ANGELA. Dad is going to do what he wants. If he wants to eat and drink himself to death no one can stop him. It's time to start your life.

MARIE. Out in the middle of nowhere?

ANGELA. Would you rather it be here?

MARIE. No. I said I want to come with you but…

ANGELA. But what?

MARIE. This bullshit about the Christening isn't fair. Why can't I just do that and come out there on Monday?

ANGELA. Because I don't want you to look at this as a "little adventure" as Dad called it.

MARIE. And bailing on Carlo and Tara changes that?

ANGELA. You'll be making a bold and honest decision and taking a stand against something.

MARIE. Against what?

ANGELA. We covered this on the phone. I don't need to say it again.

MARIE. But the problem is that I don't care. So what if I don't believe in it or Carlo doesn't believe in it. It's just one of those things that people do that doesn't matter.

ANGELA. It does matter.

MARIE. Whatever. So what's the deal? If I stand as godmother you won't let me come with you? That's it?

ANGELA. Let me ask you something. Do you remember what you said to me when I told you I was going to enlist?

MARIE. I said I was proud of you and I respected you.

ANGELA. You also said that you would never do it because you could never live a life of taking orders.

MARIE. That's right.

ANGELA. That's what you're doing.

MARIE. I'm living a life of taking orders?

ANGELA. Yes. And you know where it's going to lead you?

MARIE. I'm sure you do.

ANGELA. You'll party for about three more years. Then when you turn twenty-five, you'll meet a guy, after two years you'll get engaged, you'll marry him a year later, you'll have some kids, you'll gain fifty pounds, get an SUV, then when you're done taking the kids to little league games you'll run for Mom's assembly seat.

MARIE. You've got it all figured out, huh?

ANGELA. Come on. Let's take a walk. I'll make everything clear.

MARIE. I've been up for almost twenty-four hours and I'd like to sleep.

ANGELA. But your brain is in the best place to hear this now. It's all mushy. Come on.

(**ANGIE** *gets up but* **MARIE** *doesn't budge.*)

MARIE. You know, you act like nothing is wrong, but we all know what happened over there. You're clearly hurting. That's why you're acting out and hating on everyone.

ANGELA. I'm not hating on anyone.

MARIE. Maybe if you talked about it instead of just preaching, maybe you wouldn't be so angry. Instead we have to hear about everything from total strangers and newspapers.

ANGELA. Okay. Let's talk about it now.

MARIE. You don't have to. That's not what I meant.

ANGELA. His name was Raymond Connolly and he was from Maine. He was sweet and funny and we fell in love and had big plans. Then on March eighth his convoy was hit by an IED. He was riding in a two hundred thousand dollar humvee and he was blown to hell by five dollars worth of pennies and a nine volt battery. They sent what was left of him back to his mother in a box. His torso, a hand, a foot.

(**MARIE** *starts crying.*)

I was devastated. I couldn't eat. I couldn't sleep. I thought about killing myself but I didn't. I hung in there because I knew I was done in four months. And then they extended me. And then a few months later we were ambushed moving supplies to Baghdad. Three of us died. Seven of us were seriously injured. Melanie doesn't have legs anymore. Sandra doesn't have a face. Should I keep going? Remember what Mom looked like in her final days in the hospital? That was nothing.

MARIE. And you didn't get a scratch on you?

ANGELA. A few.

MARIE. You ever think maybe Mom was looking out for you?

ANGELA. How do you explain Raymond, Sandra or Melanie? Weren't their dead relatives looking out for them? No one's looking out for us. That's why we have to take care of ourselves. That's why I want you to leave here with me.

*(**CARLO SR.** enters the room again.)*

Don't worry we're leaving.

(The lights go down.)

End of Act I

ACT II

Scene I

(The lights come up on the kitchen. **CARLO SR.** *has moved the furniture around and he's mopping the floor.)*

(He has talk radio on, and he's in his own world.)

(JUNIOR *enters the kitchen through the back door. He carries a rolled up poster in his hand.)*

*(***CARLO SR.** *doesn't seem to notice him.)*

(JUNIOR *turns off the radio.)*

CARLO SR. Morning.

JUNIOR. It's the afternoon.

CARLO SR. Is it? I've lost track of time.

JUNIOR. You been cleaning all morning?

CARLO SR. Yeah. There's dirt and crap all over the place.

JUNIOR. Looks fine to me.

CARLO SR. That's because I've been cleaning. You should have seen it when I woke up.

JUNIOR. You in a better mood today?

CARLO SR. Yeah. You?

JUNIOR. Sure. Have you heard from Marie?

CARLO SR. No. They never came home.

JUNIOR. Did they flee into the wilderness already?

CARLO SR. Calm yourself. Marie is not going to bail on you.

JUNIOR. She's going to do whatever Angie says. You know it.

CARLO SR. I don't know anything right now. What's that in your hand?

JUNIOR. You really think Marie's going to turn down Angie's offer?

CARLO SR. We're not talking about this now.

(CARLO SR. yanks the poster out of JUNIOR's hand. He opens it.)

(It's JUNIOR's campaign poster, a clean one.)

JUNIOR. Ralph did me a solid and printed up a bunch of new ones overnight.

CARLO SR. Looks nice. Hey I'm sorry about my attitude yesterday. It was a rough day.

JUNIOR. It was a rough day for all of us.

CARLO SR. *(reading poster)* "Colletti for Congress for Change."

JUNIOR. You making fun?

CARLO SR. Of course not. You know I believe in you.

JUNIOR. I'm going to go put this up in the front.

CARLO SR. Before you do that, let me ask you a question. This whole politics thing, why do you do it?

JUNIOR. Are you joking?

CARLO SR. No. Why do you do it?

JUNIOR. You know why.

CARLO SR. Remind me.

JUNIOR. Because I want to make the world a better place. Better for you, me, my family, Marie and even Angie. Is that answer good enough?

CARLO SR. Do you think it will ever happen? This whole making the world a better place thing?

JUNIOR. Well, is the world a better place than when you grew up?

CARLO SR. In some ways. Not in others.

JUNIOR. I think it's better in most ways. And the ways that it's not, we'll change it.

CARLO SR. Do you consider yourself an optimist?

JUNIOR. Yes, I do.

CARLO SR. Do you think I'm a pessimist?

JUNIOR. No.

CARLO SR. Really? Why not?

JUNIOR. You're still here. You're still trying.

CARLO SR. What the hell does that mean? Because I'm still breathing, I'm still trying?

JUNIOR. No. But you're living your life, doing the best you can. Raising your family.

CARLO SR. Don't be a politician with me. Be honest.

JUNIOR. If you're just going to bust my chops, I'm going to go.

CARLO SR. I'm not. But I don't see how you can give me credit for the job I've done with this family.

JUNIOR. What is with you this morning? Did Angie get to you?

CARLO SR. Don't blame it on her. You're always breaking my balls, too.

JUNIOR. Only about the drinking and the eating. Just cut back on them and you'll be fine.

CARLO SR. Yeah, yeah, yeah. Are you going to be fine if Marie bails on you?

JUNIOR. I thought you said she's not going to bail.

CARLO SR. I don't think so but...

JUNIOR. But what?

CARLO SR. I want you to have a talk with Angie when she gets back.

(**JUNIOR** *laughs.*)

Don't laugh. I want her to stay here and I want you to help me make that happen.

JUNIOR. Her mind is made up. What we should do is concentrate on Marie.

CARLO SR. Marie isn't going anywhere if we get Angie to stay.

JUNIOR. Which isn't going to happen.

CARLO SR. I thought you were an optimist.

JUNIOR. I'm also a realist.

CARLO SR. Look, in order to help her, I need her to stay. And maybe if we convince her that we don't think she's crazy, she'll consider staying.

JUNIOR. You're fighting a lost cause.

CARLO SR. That's what she says you're doing with your political career...and all the rest of us with everything else.

JUNIOR. Look, I understand what you're trying to do, and don't get me wrong, I feel really bad for her with everything that's happened, but you can't rationalize her behavior.

CARLO SR. Watch a head get blown off in front of you and then talk to me.

JUNIOR. Listen to me, I'm not doubting the trauma she went through.

CARLO SR. Is going through.

JUNIOR. Fine, is going through. But to blame us for this and to lash out at us like this is...

CARLO SR. Crazy?

JUNIOR. A little bit.

CARLO SR. Do you believe that virgins can have babies?

JUNIOR. You been drinking today?

CARLO SR. Not at all actually. Now answer the question.

JUNIOR. No. It's a stupid question.

CARLO SR. So if Marie were to walk in here and tell us that she's pregnant but swear to God that she's a virgin, you wouldn't believe her?

JUNIOR. I think we both know Marie is not a virgin.

CARLO SR. I'm speaking hypothetically.

JUNIOR. Of course I wouldn't believe her, and I know where you're going with this. You want to know why I'm raising my kids Catholic, if I don't really believe that virgins can have babies.

CARLO SR. So your answer is no?

JUNIOR. Angie's gotten to you, hasn't she?

CARLO SR. So you're raising your kids in a religion that is based entirely on something you don't believe could ever happen?

JUNIOR. Okay, well, let me ask you, why did you raise us in it if you didn't believe in it?

CARLO SR. I really didn't give a shit. Your mother wanted it.

JUNIOR. Did she really believe in it?

CARLO SR. I don't know. We never talked about it. We were both raised Catholic so we just did it. Maybe we should've discussed it. Maybe you and Tara should too.

JUNIOR. You want us to discuss leaving the church?

CARLO SR. What are you afraid of? Do you think it will hurt your election chances?

JUNIOR. Come on. We're not Catholic just to win elections, and I highly doubt that's why mom was.

CARLO SR. Of course not. A lot of people go through the motions with religion and they're not running for office. But let's be honest, if it got around you think it's all bullshit, you'd never win an election around here.

JUNIOR. I never said it was ALL bullshit.

CARLO SR. But you know it is. I know it is. And you know what, if they thought about it, deep down, most people would admit it's all crazy. Yet they wouldn't vote for you if you ever admit to that. Ain't that something?

JUNIOR. Dad, enough. It's not all crazy. There's nothing crazy about teaching kids about a peaceful, gentle man who loves them and looks out for them and teaches good things. That's why we do it, okay? Now of course if we took everything literally, we'd have to admit it's crazy. But we're not talking about all of it. Having faith in something that you can't see, feel, or prove is okay. It doesn't mean you have to go to the extremes like the nuts do. You don't have to choose between being an atheist or a nut. You don't have to believe that there's no God, and you don't have to believe that the earth is only five thousand years old, or that dinosaurs didn't exist, or that a man lived in a whale. Now that's crazy.

CARLO SR. Is it any crazier than believing in a virgin birth? Or some guy believing that seventy-two virgins are his if he kills in the name of Allah?

JUNIOR. One is a dangerous extreme, the other is a harmless leap of faith.

CARLO SR. Do you remember the old Winston Churchill joke? The one where he asks a woman if she'll have sex with him for a thousand dollars and she says yes. Then he asks her if she'll do it for five dollars and she says, "What kind of a woman do you think I am?" Then he says, "We've already established what kind of woman, now we're just haggling over the price."

JUNIOR. I think Churchill would've said pounds.

CARLO SR. It doesn't matter. Do you get my point?

JUNIOR. It's not the strongest metaphor I've ever heard, but I get your point. But I don't think it's the same. Using a "sacred text" to justify murder is different than using it to justify wrapping presents and putting up a tree.

CARLO SR. It's more destructive and evil sure but no more irrational or crazy. Believing in one absurd tale justifies belief in all absurd tales, no?

JUNIOR. So are you calling me a religious extremist?

CARLO SR. Of course not. But your lifestyle does fuel their fire, doesn't it?

JUNIOR. They want to force their religion on others. I believe in the separation of church and state. That's how I'm different. So stop this. And I advise you to not talk this way in front of Angie. You'll only enable her craziness.

CARLO SR. You're the one who's raising his kids in a faith you don't believe in. Which one of you is crazier?

JUNIOR. She's talking about unplugging from society to live in a log cabin in the middle of nowhere!

CARLO SR. It's a bit extreme but…

JUNIOR. Go with her then.

CARLO SR. I'm not going with her. I want her to stay here.

JUNIOR. And I want to be President of the United States. What do you want me to tell you?

CARLO SR. Don't tell me anything. Admit to her that you agree with her on all this.

JUNIOR. But I don't.

CARLO SR. Then lie to her. You've lied to get votes sometimes, right?

JUNIOR. Don't you get this yet? It won't matter what I say. She has some kind of vendetta against me. She blames me for a war that started when I was in grad school for Christsake.

(Voices are heard offstage.)

(HUTCH, carrying MARIE in a piggy back ride, enters the kitchen through the backyard door.)

HUTCH. Mr. C! Good morning, sir!

CARLO SR. It's afternoon.

(MARIE hops off of HUTCH's back and kisses CARLO SR. on the cheek.)

MARIE. Hi, Daddy.

CARLO SR. You guys smell like a gin mill.

HUTCH. That's because we've been drinking all night.

CARLO SR. Really?

(JUNIOR gets right in HUTCH's face.)

HUTCH. What's up, face?

JUNIOR. If you vandalize my posters again I'll have you arrested and you know I can get it done.

HUTCH. Colletti for Congress for...cock. You don't like that?

JUNIOR. You got me?

(CARLO SR. grabs HUTCH by the back of the neck.)

CARLO SR. Out of my house now.

HUTCH. I'm leaving.

MARIE. Yeah. Just go. You have to pack.

(**MARIE** *starts to fix herself a glass of whiskey.*)

HUTCH. Mr. C, if I went to Colorado would you miss me?

JUNIOR. You'd be depriving this village of a pretty good idiot.

CARLO SR. Out!

HUTCH. Okay. I can see when I'm not wanted.

MARIE. Remember, the train is at six eleven!

HUTCH. Copy that.

JUNIOR. *(to* **MARIE***)* What was that?

MARIE. What was what?

(*While Carlo's attention is on* **MARIE**, **HUTCH** *grabs a poster off of the table and runs to the door.*)

HUTCH. I got your face, face!

(**JUNIOR** *starts to pursue, but* **CARLO SR.** *stops him.*)

CARLO SR. Let it go.

(**CARLO SR.** *walks over to* **MARIE**, *takes her drink and pours it in the sink.*)

MARIE. It's okay for you to drink in the morning but not me?

CARLO SR. It's the afternoon and you're already drunk. Where's Angie?

MARIE. She'll be here soon, she's just tying up some loose ends. And I'm going to sleep.

(**MARIE** *moves towards the livingroom door.*)

CARLO SR. You sit your ass down.

MARIE. But I haven't slept in almost forty-eight hours now!

CARLO SR. That's you're own fault. Now sit.

(**CARLO SENIOR** *leads her to a chair, with very little resistance.*)

(**JUNIOR** *gets in her face.*)

JUNIOR. You listen to me, if you bail on me –

CARLO SR. Carlo, shut up.

(He pulls CARLO away from her.)

MARIE. Yeah. Shut up.

JUNIOR. Don't tell me to shut up. You agreed to be godmother and now it's three days before the fucking Christening and you're bailing.

MARIE. Do you really want me? I know you know I'm a bad Catholic.

CARLO SR. Let's not do one of these, okay?

MARIE. It's true. Dad, whenever I tell you that I passed out on the train and wound up in Ronkonkoma, that's code for, "I was in someone's apartment being a bad Catholic." I don't think I need to go into anymore detail, do I?

CARLO SR. Is this the liquor talking?

JUNIOR. It's Angie talking.

MARIE. Oh no, this is me. I'm not a good Catholic, none of us are. Not even you, Carlo. You're pro-choice, pro-gay rights, pro-contraception but apparently not good at it and you were quite the "player" before you met Tara, weren't you? So why don't we just drop the whole thing? You don't really believe in any of it.

JUNIOR. I believe in some of it, okay? I don't have to believe in all of it.

MARIE. Really? So the parts of the Bible that you like are God's laws but the parts you don't like are bullshit?

(JUNIOR laughs in disbelief. CARLO SR. puts his arm around him and leads him to a seat.)

JUNIOR. I'm just getting it from all ends this week.

CARLO SR. Relax, relax. Let me get you a drink.

MARIE. Oh he can have a drink and I can't?

CARLO SR. Fine. I'll make you both drinks. We can pretend we're in a bar. And you know what else we do in bars? We don't talk religion.

(CARLO SR. fixes whiskeys for JUNIOR and MARIE, but not for himself.)

MARIE. Aren't we discussing a Christening?

CARLO SR. Not anymore. You don't want to do it, you don't do it. Carlo will find someone else.

JUNIOR. With three days to go?

CARLO SR. Drink your whiskey, Carlo. Alright, honey, listen up, yesterday you promised me you wouldn't add to any drama.

MARIE. You don't really want to get into a battle of broken promises, do you?

CARLO SR. Okay, fair enough. My point is that Angie is not well, and we need her to stay here so she can get well.

MARIE. You're going to help her get well? You?

CARLO SR. We all will.

MARIE. Oh please. She's not even sick. Talk to her.

CARLO SR. I have.

JUNIOR. We all have.

CARLO SR. And she has some issues.

MARIE. Don't we all?

CARLO SR. Yes, but her's are a little more complicated.

MARIE. Maybe her's are actually pretty simple. She just sees through the bullshit.

JUNIOR. Oh Christ, you too?

CARLO SR. Carlo, shut up.

MARIE. Seriously. What's so crazy about what she's saying?

JUNIOR. I swear to God, I'm about to tear this kitchen apart to look for the candid camera! You've all had one whiskey too many. Why don't all three of you go and start your own nuthouse in Colorado?

MARIE. It's a lot easier to label her crazy than it is to think about what she has to say.

JUNIOR. We've all thought about what she said.

MARIE. Have you thought about how you're making a pledge to fight for women's equality in the military, yet you're baptizing your daughters into an organization that sees them as second class citizens?

JUNIOR. Oh here we go.

MARIE. How many female Popes have there been? Tell me where I'm wrong.

JUNIOR. You're wrong.

MARIE. Tell me why.

JUNIOR. Angie is crazy and you're even crazier if you go with her.

MARIE. Or is it crazier to stay here and live a life like yours?

JUNIOR. What is wrong with my life? Is there something wrong with living a slightly traditional lifestyle? Holy shit! When did everyone lose their fucking minds?

MARIE. But you don't believe in any of those traditions.

(*JUNIOR approaches her and puts his hands all over her head as if he's looking for something.*)

JUNIOR. Did she put a remote control in your head?

MARIE. Get your hands off me.

(*She shoves him away.* **CARLO SR.** *steps between them and restores order.*)

CARLO SR. Leave her alone. Alright, are you just breaking balls or are you really leaving?

MARIE. I don't know.

CARLO SR. The clock is ticking.

(*JUNIOR approaches MARIE.*)

JUNIOR. I'll make this real simple for you. Forget it. I'll get someone else.

MARIE. Is that the way you want it?

JUNIOR. Yes it is. I'm done. This is such bullshit.

CARLO SR. You're right, Carlo, now sit down.

JUNIOR. I'm out of here.

(*He starts for the door.* **CARLO SR.** *follows.*)

CARLO SR. I want you to talk to Angie.

JUNIOR. No.

CARLO SR. Come on. I need your help. She's your sister.

(**JUNIOR** *leaves out the back and slams the door again.*)

CARLO SR. *(cont.)* Alright, he's gone. Now cut the bullshit. What's going on?

MARIE. I told you. I'm not sure.

CARLO SR. What you're doing is wrong. You want to go, go. If you don't, you call Carlo right now.

MARIE. Don't put a deadline on me. I will make the choice I want to make.

CARLO SR. It sounds like your mind is made up. You're with Angie.

MARIE. I agree with what she has to say, yes. But I'm not "with" her.

CARLO SR. What do you mean?

MARIE. I think the things she's saying are right, but she's on some kind of mission. And I don't want to spend my life on a mission.

CARLO SR. So while we're on the subject, how about you tell me what you do want?

MARIE. I'm not sure. But I'll tell you what else I don't want. I don't want to spend anymore of my life watching you die. I think watching Mom go was enough, don't you?

CARLO SR. Honey –

MARIE. Don't "honey" me. If the next couple of years are going to be like the last year and a half, then I'd rather be with Angie. And if the only way she's going to let me come is to bail on a bullshit Christening, then I will. I'll feel bad for Carlo and Tara, but…too bad. They have their own life, you've had yours, and I'm entitled to mine.

CARLO SR. So what do you want from me?

MARIE. I want you to start doing what I say.

CARLO SR. That's it?

MARIE. No, no, no. Don't try to pull one over on me. Don't try and behave through the weekend and then go back to boozing and eating yourself to death on Monday.

CARLO SR. Well…I haven't had a drink yet today.

MARIE. But you'll have one later?

CARLO SR. Very likely. But I'll try again tomorrow. And the day after that. And the day after that. And that's the best I can do.

MARIE. Bullshit. You just don't want to do better. The results speak for themselves. If you were really trying, you wouldn't be in the shape you're in.

CARLO SR. What do you know at twenty-two?

MARIE. I know that every time we get hit with something hard, you go in the tank. Every time. When Mom died. When we found out about what happened to Angie. You can't take it. You can't deal.

CARLO SR. I got news for you, if I didn't want to try anymore, I would flat-out kill myself. I wouldn't do it slowly like this. I'd blow my goddamn brains out. So get some life experience under your belt instead of some frat-boy and maybe you'd understand.

(She gets right in his face.)

MARIE. I can't believe you just said that.

CARLO SR. I'm sorry, honey. I didn't mean that.

MARIE. Fuck you.

CARLO SR. I deserved that. You've had to grow up with me for a father, and your mom's passing and now all of this. That's plenty of life experience. I shouldn't treat you like a child.

MARIE. Don't ever say anything like that to me again.

CARLO SR. I won't. So I guess you should start packing.

(He moves away from her. She stands her ground.)

MARIE. Why did you say you were going to blow your brains out?

CARLO SR. I never said that. I've had a gun for forty years. If I was going to do something like that, wouldn't I have done it a long time ago?

MARIE. What's going to happen when Angie and I leave? Are you going to put on your old Army uniform and blow your head off?

CARLO SR. You've watched too many movies.

MARIE. I want you to give it to me.

CARLO SR. Get out of here. I'm not giving you my gun.

MARIE. I know where it is. I'll get it myself.

CARLO SR. I moved it along with all of my whiskey.

MARIE. Give it to me.

CARLO SR. Over my dead body.

MARIE. Which isn't going to be long, is it?

CARLO SR. That gun is here to protect us.

MARIE. There's no reason for it to be here. Say goodbye to it or say goodbye to me.

(They stare each other down for a beat.)

CARLO SR. Fine.

MARIE. Fine?

CARLO SR. You heard me.

MARIE. Good. Tomorrow then, before I go to work.

CARLO SR. What?

MARIE. You heard me. I'm going to call Carlo and tell him that as long as we get rid of your gun tomorrow, I'm staying and I will be godmother. We'll all go together.

CARLO SR. Sounds good.

MARIE. And no more drinking either and I will now do ALL the food shopping.

CARLO SR. You're getting the gun, that's plenty. Don't push your luck.

MARIE. You're giving up the booze and the junk food too, or I'm gone.

CARLO SR. So you want an unconditional surrender?

MARIE. You had a good run. It's time.

(ANGELA enters from outside.)

CARLO SR. I think your sister has something to tell you.

MARIE. Do I?

CARLO SR. Yes. You're the boss.

ANGELA. Let me guess. You're not coming with me?

MARIE. He said he'd kill himself if I went.

ANGELA. Oh Christ.

CARLO SR. I did not. I told her that if I was going to kill myself I would've done it years ago.

MARIE. You weren't here. You didn't hear him. You also didn't hear him say he was going to screw his head on right if I stay.

ANGELA. And you believe him? He's trying to manipulate you into staying. Apparently it's working.

MARIE. He's serious this time.

ANGELA. Look, if you don't want to come, don't. But this is the wrong reason. Do something for yourself. Do –

MARIE. I'll do what I feel is right. Now, I am finally going to get some fucking sleep!

(MARIE gets in CARLO's face.)

Do not, I repeat, do not break this promise to me.

ANGELA. Marie!

MARIE. I have to go to bed. I'll see you before you go.

(MARIE leaves the room.)

(ANGELA looks at CARLO.)

CARLO SR. You really turned this place upside down. Are you happy?

ANGELA. Do I look happy?

CARLO SR. This is what you wanted?

ANGELA. I wanted my little sister to take a different path.

CARLO SR. You failed.

ANGELA. At least I tried.

CARLO SR. You know, you may still decide to have kids one day, and when you do –

ANGELA. I'll teach them to use their brains and think for themselves. And that's the only moral way to raise a kid, so save your breath.

(She leaves the room.)

(The lights go down.)

Scene II

(The lights come up.)

(ANGELA sits at the table, rearranging some things into her huge duffle bag.)

(JUNIOR enters through the back door.)

(They lock eyes, but say nothing.)

(He gives her an envelope.)

(She opens it. It's a pile of cash.)

ANGELA. I don't want your money.

JUNIOR. Just a little something to help. Put it in there.

ANGELA. I'll be fine without it. Thank you.

(She hands the envelope back to him. He doesn't accept it.)

JUNIOR. I insist.

ANGELA. I insist that you use it on your children.

JUNIOR. Don't you worry about my children. I can take care of them.

ANGELA. I don't doubt it, but I do not need, nor do I want your money.

(She throws the envelope on the table.)

JUNIOR. What is your problem with me?

ANGELA. Have we ever really been friends? Be honest.

JUNIOR. We don't have to be friends. We're family.

ANGELA. Exactly. So what's the point?

JUNIOR. The point is that I love you and –

ANGELA. But would you really love me if we didn't have the same parents?

JUNIOR. Take the damn money and call if you need me.

(He tosses the envelope back at her.)

(He starts for the living room door.)

ANGELA. If you leave this here, I'm just going to leave it with Dad.

(He snatches it from her.)

JUNIOR. What would you say if I said I wanted to come with you? What if I told you that I'm not in love with Tara anymore, or that I made a mistake by having kids, and that I'm ready to chuck it all and join you out there?

ANGELA. Are you?

JUNIOR. Don't you think I've thought about it? Don't you think that on some days when it all just gets to be too much, and the babies are screaming and crying, and I'm getting hate mail, and I have work people calling me, and Tara calling me, and Dad is on a drinking binge, and Marie doesn't show up to watch the kids, and…don't you think I just want to get in my car and drive and go where no one can find me? Well, I do.

ANGELA. Why don't you do it then?

JUNIOR. What would it accomplish?

ANGELA. What are you accomplishing now?

JUNIOR. I'm working. I'm trying to change things. I'm trying to –

ANGELA. You're changing nothing.

JUNIOR. Will you stop that? Okay. Do you want me to admit that I think you're right about a lot? Well you are. Things are fucked. And people like me are not the problem. People like you are. People who just rail against politicians. And yes, most of us do suck. But some of us are doing everything we can to make this sick world a better place. Some of us are trying to keep what happened to you from happening to anyone else. And we can use a little support. Not just criticism and insults every step of the way. In order to change things, yes, I have to compromise. I have to play the game a little. I have to break a few rules to get there. I have to pretend to support things I don't believe in. I have to tell a few lies. I don't like it anymore than you do. But if I don't, I'll never get inside. And if I never get inside, I can't fight for change. Right now, I can't overplay my hand.

ANGELA. Every idealistic, young politician has said that, but nothing changes. You know why? Because people will always want their bullshit comforts. God and country. So you'll change nothing from the "inside."

JUNIOR. Well look who's in the White House. That looks like change to me. You don't think so?

ANGELA. We'll see how much he changes things.

(**JUNIOR** *takes a step away from her. He calms himself and collects his thoughts.*)

JUNIOR. Maybe if you presented your points in a less aggressive way, people would listen to you.

ANGELA. It really wouldn't matter. I think deep down you know it.

JUNIOR. You know, when we were young, and we both talked about entering politics, I always knew it was you who was going to be the successful one. You were the one who was going to soar past mom's accomplishments and anything I could ever achieve. You had a way of connecting with people and everyone loved you and listened to you and you never seemed fake or phony. I used to be so threatened by it. I used to resent you for it. And now I'd give anything to see that again. Now that I'm older, I realize how important that quality is. I don't have it and I never will. And it's sad because you're the one who can make a difference with people. Not me. It's something Mom and Dad always knew. We all did.

ANGELA. What can I tell you? I guess I left it over there.

JUNIOR. I don't think you did. I think you just refuse to use it.

ANGELA. I have my reasons.

JUNIOR. I know. I'm not judging you. I'm just asking you one more time to join me. Come on. Help me out. Stand by my side. We can make a difference. We can do it. You coach me on being more sincere and I'll coach you on being less aggressive. It will work. We will make the change.

ANGELA. Starting the Colletti political dynasty? The Kennedys of Long Island?

JUNIOR. Well, let's avoid the scandals and the corruption and such. And this place is a shithole compared to the Kennedy compound, but we have to start somewhere.

ANGELA. *(she laughs)* Mom's dream. You don't give up, do you?

JUNIOR. I never will. Nor should you. Let's do it.

ANGELA. I'll tell you what, you go win that Congressional seat, and I'll come out of Colorado and join you once you've changed the world.

JUNIOR. But then I'll never see you again.

ANGELA. Exactly.

JUNIOR. I was joking. I was making a joke.

> (**HUTCH** *shows up at the back door. He knocks and enters.*)

ANGELA. Hey!

> (**HUTCH** *doesn't even look at* **JUNIOR**.)

JUNIOR. I'm going to go get Marie.

> (**JUNIOR** *leaves the kitchen.*)

> (**ANGELA** *gives* **HUTCH** *a big kiss. As they separate, she holds his hands.*)

> (*He doesn't say anything. She finally notices the look on his face.*)

ANGELA. What's wrong?

HUTCH. Nothing. I have a great idea. Instead of doing this Colorado thing, what do you say we stay here and move in together?

ANGELA. Move in together?

HUTCH. Hell yeah!

ANGELA. Why can't we just go to Colorado?

HUTCH. It's better if we get a place here and move in together.

ANGELA. Oh God.

HUTCH. Come on. We can pick up where we left off and –

ANGELA. That's what I want to do.

HUTCH. But our families are here. Our friends are here.

ANGELA. And they always will be.

HUTCH. Come on. We can get a place. We can get jobs. We can have fun. We can –

ANGELA. I can't believe this.

HUTCH. I'm sorry to disappoint you. But I just had to do some hardcore thinking, and I just don't see this as a good idea.

ANGELA. Just try it for a little while. If you're not happy after a few months, you can come back and I won't be mad. I promise.

HUTCH. I'll lose my job.

ANGELA. You can get another job like that and you know it.

HUTCH. Angie, I don't want to go.

ANGELA. For all of your talk about how much you hate it around here and about recognizing all the bullshit, it's all just talk, isn't it? You're afraid to just walk away.

HUTCH. It's not all talk and I'm not afraid to walk away. I like being one of the only ones who sees through all the bullshit. I get a kick out of fucking with all the drones around here and I want to continue breaking their balls. Stay here and we won't be like everyone else. We won't get married. We won't have kids. We'll go around and raise hell. We'll be the town drunks. We'll sabotage political campaigns. I really don't care, but I just want to be with you, and I want to be here. We can be two lunatics terrorizing Long Island.

(**JUNIOR** and **MARIE** enter the kitchen. **HUTCH** and **ANGIE** don't acknowledge them.)

HUTCH. Just because I don't want to unplug doesn't mean I love everything about Hicksville. But it's not so god-awful that abandoning it is the only way to deal with it. My way is more fun. I'm telling you. We can do this. We can be happy here. You can be happy here. Give that a chance. Me and you.

ANGELA. This was supposed to be so simple, Hutch. All I wanted was to come back here and bring you home with me. You have nothing going on here.

HUTCH. I will if you stay. And you will if you stay with me. Remember what happened last time you didn't take my advice?

(She takes his hands.)

ANGELA. Please come with me. Please.

HUTCH. Please stay.

(She jerks her hands back.)

ANGELA. Get out of here.

HUTCH. Angie, don't be like that. I –

ANGELA. Get the fuck out!

(She shoves him and turns around.)

*(She notices **JUNIOR** and **MARIE** and quickly composes himself.)*

HUTCH. You'll know where to find me. I'm not going anywhere, Ang.

(He leaves.)

*(She watches him go. She keeps her back to **MARIE** and **CARLO**.)*

JUNIOR. You okay?

ANGELA. I'm fine.

JUNIOR. You sure?

*(**ANGELA** turns around and nods.)*

*(**MARIE** puts a letter on the table.)*

MARIE. Please don't open it until I go.

ANGELA. Still trying to get me to stay?

MARIE. No. Are you sure you want to go?

*(**ANGELA** hugs her and gives her a sisterly pat on the head.)*

I really admire you for this. I just can't do it. I hope you're not mad at me.

ANGELA. No. Love you.

MARIE. Love you too.

*(She breaks the hug with **MARIE** and picks up the letter.)*

*(She stands in front of **JUNIOR**.)*

JUNIOR. Why don't you give it few more days and –

*(She hugs **JUNIOR**, quickly and tightly, then she darts out of the room.)*

(He seems a little shocked by it.)

*(**MARIE** is visibly upset, **JUNIOR** puts his arm around her.)*

Come on. Come play with the kids for a bit. It will take your mind off of things.

(They leave.)

(The lights go down.)

Scene III

(The lights come up.)

(CARLO SR. sits at the table with a small leather bag in front of him.)

(ANGIE enters the room.)

(She stops at the door and doesn't approach him.)

CARLO SR. You out of here?

ANGELA. My train leaves in twenty minutes.

CARLO SR. Okay. So I guess this is it.

(CARLO SR. pulls an envelope out of the bag. He tosses it to her.)

ANGELA. I don't want your money.

CARLO SR. You may need it.

ANGELA. Carlo tried this, too. Did you put him up to it?

CARLO SR. No, and I'm a little surprised actually. But you are taking this money.

ANGELA. Dad –

CARLO SR. Put it in your bag.

ANGELA. Fine. Anything else?

(He pulls a gun out of the little bag.)

ANGELA. I have my own. Besides, I'm going to Colorado not Beirut.

(She hands it back to him. He doesn't accept it back.)

CARLO SR. But I want you to have this one.

ANGELA. That's ridiculous. Keep it.

CARLO SR. Your sister's making me get rid of it anyway. Take it.

ANGELA. No.

(She puts it on the kitchen table. She picks up the envelope and puts it in her bag.)

CARLO SR. I know you want to try and live off the grid and all that, but put the money in the bank and get yourself an ATM card. Don't carry it all around with you.

ANGELA. Of course.

CARLO SR. Well, take care of yourself and stay in touch.

(She starts for the door.)

*(**CARLO** turns around, doesn't watch her leave.)*

(She stops before she gets to the door.)

ANGELA. I have something for you.

(She pulls a wrapped gift out of her bag, something tiny. It's just a little box.)

(She puts it on the table.)

CARLO SR. Let me open it before you go.

ANGELA. I have to get moving.

(She starts for the door again.)

(He picks up the gift, but he doesn't open it. He puts it down.)

(She gets to the door.)

CARLO SR. I know exactly how you feel.

(That stops her.)

They treated us like shit when I was in the service, too. They paid us like shit. Our hospitals were shit. And when we got home, no one liked us. No one cared. You've heard the stories about what it was like for us to come home. You know.

ANGELA. But I never heard these stories from you. Only from other people, movies, books. And when I asked you about it, you would always blow it off and still make it clear that you still worship your country, like a battered wife to her husband.

CARLO SR. Please. Let me make my point. Let *ME* do some preaching. My point is that nowadays, at least now they call you guys heroes. They love you now.

ANGELA. Just because they put "I support the troops" stickers on their cars doesn't mean they give a shit.

CARLO SR. But it's something. It's a step. It's change.

ANGELA. It's nothing. And it only gets most, or some of us, more upset.

CARLO SR. Why don't we do something about it?

ANGELA. I am.

CARLO SR. No you're not. This is not the answer. All this shit got to me too and when I got back I was confused –

ANGELA. I know. And you wandered around just like I did and –

CARLO SR. Not really.

ANGELA. Not really?

CARLO SR. Well, I did for a little bit, for a few weeks. But after wandering around and not finding what I was looking for, I checked myself into a hospital.

ANGELA. I considered that too.

CARLO SR. I'm sure. I spent a lot of days and nights with a gun in my hand. Each day I got a little bit closer to using it. And as I got really close, I decided to go get help.

ANGELA. So was Marie right? Did you threaten to kill yourself?

CARLO SR. Of course not. I was simply trying to tell her what I'm telling you. That I know how strongly you must feel, but you can't give up.

ANGELA. I'm giving up? You're giving up. You've given up. You gave up when you came home! You could've changed something. You could've spoken out. You would've taught us differently. But you decided to keep all those "bad" feelings and everything you learned and went through to yourself. You just did what everyone else did.

(She approaches him.)

Why didn't you tell me? Why didn't you sit me down and say, "Honey, if you go, the worst thing that will happen to you is that you'll be dead. And the best thing that will happen is that you'll come back a shell of your former self? And when you do come home, some people will hate you, some will claim they love you, but none of them really care." Why didn't you say something?

(**CARLO** *says nothing.*)

ANGELA. *(cont.)* Answer me!

CARLO SR. I just didn't think it would happen to you. I…I'm so sorry. I…

(He goes to hug her, she shoves him away.)

ANGELA. Everyday I think about how things would be different. What if I had never enlisted? I would have never met Raymond…or lost him. I would have never seen those bodies.

(She begins to break down.)

I wouldn't have these nightmares every night. If I had just come home after college I would be married right now. I'd have a baby. Marie would be godmother. I'd be running for Mom's assembly seat. I'd be on a poster with Carlo. My kids would be playing with his kids. I'd be raising my kids the same way you raised us. The same way your parents raised you. We'd be mom's dream. And we'd be so fucking happy we wouldn't know what to do with ourselves. There's a side of me that wishes I could erase all of it, just turn it off and be like everyone else. Just be happy as a little cog in the big machine. But I can't do it now. Oh God….I just want it to go away. I just want it gone.

(She's a mess. **CARLO** *holds her. She allows it this time.)*

(He leads her to a seat.)

CARLO SR. It never will go away. You'll just learn how to live with it. It doesn't matter how many therapists you see or how much medication you take. You just have to get used to it. And you will.

ANGELA. There are moments that I feel like it's gone. And then there are moments it comes roaring back.

CARLO SR. I know. I've been dealing with it for forty years.

ANGELA. Why didn't you stop me?

CARLO SR. I wish I could go back now and do it all over. I wish I could raise all of you differently. But I can't. All we have is now. And all we can do is make the best of it. So now I'm going to stop you. You're staying here. I will help you through this.

(He picks up her bag and moves it away from the door.)

We'll deal with the pain. And then we'll do what I never did. We'll do what my parents and their parents never did. We'll make sure no one ever goes through what we went through. We'll find who you were. We'll find who I was. We'll change things.

(She seems to be calming down a little.)

ANGELA. How are we going to do that?

CARLO SR. I don't know. We'll figure it out. We can speak out. We can tell people what we've been through. We can tell them how we feel and talk to them about everything you've been saying. Maybe we're the ones who can get through to them.

ANGELA. What do you think they will say?

CARLO SR. What do you say we find out?

(She puts her hands on his face and shakes her head.)

ANGELA. Dad, you just don't get it yet, do you?

CARLO SR. What? What don't I get?

ANGELA. They don't care.

CARLO SR. Yes they do. They just need to be told.

ANGELA. They don't want to hear our stories. They don't want to see the pictures. They don't want to know the truth. We fight, we suffer, and we die. They get to keep living their safe little lives. That's just how they want it.

CARLO SR. That's right, and that's what makes us soldiers. We can take it. They can't. We're tougher. We're better. We face what they can't in order to make the world a better place. So let's do it again. Let's fight a new battle. People will listen to us, especially to you.

ANGELA. Dad, they do not want us to make them think! They just want us to smile and wave the flag and make them feel like they are part of the fight. They want us to validate their patriotism, their real religion. That's what makes us "heroes" to them. It's why they live. The minute we go against what they believe in, they'll hate us. Our service will be worthless.

CARLO SR. We can take that. And we can change that.

ANGELA. You should know better at your age.

CARLO SR. Look, since you were a little girl, you've wanted to make a difference in this world. That's why you enlisted, and you suffered for it. So let's make some good from it. Don't give up now or it's going to bother you for the rest of your life. I know. That pain inside of you is only going to get worse. It's the same pain inside of me. Let's do something about it. I want to get back in the fight. I want to....watch this...

(He runs over to the liquor cabinet and pulls out a bottle of whiskey. He starts pouring it down the sink, but he keeps his eyes on **ANGELA**. *She's not looking at him.)*

(He stops emptying, leaving just a little bit in there.)

(He approaches her.)

You're going to get up there and face these people with me. We're going to fight.

(She collects herself, wiping her final tears.)

(She stands up and faces him. She takes his hand.)

ANGELA. I'm through fighting. I'm retired.

(She grabs her bag and starts for the door again.)

CARLO SR. Please don't go. All I want is a chance to fix things. It's all I'm asking for.

ANGELA. If you really believe everything you said, you can do it without me.

CARLO SR. I can't do it by myself. And trust me, you're not going to ease the pain out there by yourself. But we can do it together here, with family.

(She stops at the door.)

ANGELA. I love you, Daddy. I really do.

CARLO SR. I love you, too.

(She darts out the door before he can say anything else, leaving him alone.)

(He turns away from the door in disbelief.)

(She's gone.)

(He sits at the table.)

*(He notices **ANGELA**'s gift on the table, next to the gun.)*

(He picks it up the gift and opens it.)

(He pulls it out. He holds it up.)

(It's a set of dog tags.)

(He stares at it.)

(He breaks down.)

(He's losing it.)

(He gets up from the table. He paces as if he has no idea what to do.)

(He grabs the whiskey bottle.)

(He looks at it for a second.)

(He wipes a tear from his eye.)

(He pours the rest in the sink and puts the bottle down.)

(He goes to the table.)

(He picks up the gun.)

(He's still emotional.)

(He puts the gun back in the leather bag. He puts it down on the table.)

(He takes a breath, wiping the final tears. He straightens his posture.)

(He walks over to the phone. He picks up the cordless and dials.)

CARLO SR. Hello, Tara. How are you? I know...I know... It's a shame. Can you put Carlo...oh no...I don't think so. I'm not really hungry...I...is Marie still over there? Okay...well...you know what? Don't worry about putting him on, I'm just going to come over. Why not?... Sure...I'll be there in about ten minutes. Okay. Okay. See you soon.

(He hangs up and puts the phone down.)

(He goes back to the table. He places the dog tags back in the box and closes it.)

(He places the gift in the center of the table.)

(He looks at it with a perplexing look.)

(He grabs the leather bag and stashes it in the cabinet. He grabs his car keys.)

(He takes one last look at the gift in the center of the table.)

(He leaves out the back door, shutting the door behind him.)

(The lights go down.)

Also by
Matt Morillo...

All Aboard the Marriage Hearse

Angry Young Women in Low-Rise Jeans with High-Class Issues

Please visit our website **samuelfrench.com** for complete descriptions and licensing information.

OTHER TITLES AVAILABLE FROM SAMUEL FRENCH

ALL ABOARD THE MARRIAGE HEARSE

Matt Morillo

Dramatic Comedy / 1m, 1f / Simple Set

Sean and Amy are your typical co-habitating, Catholic/Jewish, twenty-something couple living in Manhattan. They work hard, love each other and share common goals in life. Well, sort of. After nearly three years together, Amy wants to get married but Sean does not believe in the institution. The game is on!!! Tonight is the night when they will settle the marriage question once and for all. They will both bring their "A" game and the gloves will come off. Sean will try to talk her out of it. Amy will try to talk him into it. Will they break up? Will they keep going on the path they're on? Will they climb aboard the "Marriage Hearse?" It's the perfect show for anyone who has ever been married, will be married, wants to be married, doesn't want to be married, has thought about getting married, has been told they should be married, knows someone who is married, knows someone who wants to be married, knows someone who was married, knows someone who should be married, knows someone who shouldn't be married, has parents who are married, has parents who were married, has parents who shouldn't be married, and everyone else! What else would you expect from the team that brought you *Angry Young Women In Low-Rise Jeans With High-Class Issues*?

SAMUELFRENCH.COM

OTHER TITLES AVAILABLE FROM SAMUEL FRENCH

ANGRY YOUNG WOMEN IN LOW-RISE JEANS WITH HIGH-CLASS ISSUES

Matt Morillo

Comedy / 6m, 7f (flexible casting if actors play multiple roles) / Simple Sets

This outrageous new comedy is told in five outrageously funny parts all dealing with young women and the various issues they confront today. It's part sit-com, part stand-up, and part sketch-comedy. This collection of vignettes parades a series of foxy, witty, and anxious women who bear the expectations of the world like an itchy muffler. Coffee-driven, sensitive, wired, misunderstood, and fuming with awkward issues, these girls are frustrated with the ways of the world, the perceptions men have of them and their own complex reactions to it. How, for example, do you resolve societal contradictions like dressing sexy and still considering yourself a feminist? These women go head to head with such issues as Electra complexes, bikini waxes, low rider jeans, their oversexed mothers, thongs, brazen teenagers, men's sexual fantasies, side-effects of birth control drugs, mean teenagers on the subway, sympathy sex, and the artistic integrity of penises and vaginas in independent films. This play has great material for scene and monologue work as well as for performance.

CPSIA information can be obtained at www.ICGtesting.com
Printed in the USA
LVOW130230060712

288986LV00006B/4/P